Mills & Boon Classics

A chance to read and collect some of the best-loved novels from Mills & Boon – the world's largest publisher of romantic fiction.

Every month, four titles by favourite Mills & Boon authors will be re-published in the *Classics* series.

A list of other titles in the *Classics* series can be found at the end of this book.

Margaret Way

THE TIME OF
THE JACARANDA

MILLS & BOON LIMITED
LONDON · TORONTO

First published 1970
Reprinted 1979

© Margaret Way
Australian copyright 1979
Philippine copyright 1979

ISBN 0 263 73203 7

Filmset in 10 on 11pt Plantin

*Made and printed in Great Britain by
C. Nicholls & Company Ltd
The Philips Park Press, Manchester*

CHAPTER ONE

OCTOBER sunshine rolled down from the hills, flooding the valley with liquid gold. This was the time when Saranga was its most beautiful, the heady time when everything flowered and even the pastures responded in sweet fragrant ripples. As far as the eye could see, from the purple tree-furred hills to the rich river flats, everything glistened, rustled, shone. One good season had followed another and the land continued remarkably green, blue-green, grey-green, green with a myriad of shadings. Birds shrilled in a brilliant sky, wheeling high over the paddocks smothered in daisies, as dazzling in their fashion as anything in Saranga's home gardens. The sun was full on them now, lending every leaf, every flower, its own special radiance. Contentment hung palpable in the warm scented air and gathered in intensity over the homestead.

The smooth green lawns and formal gardens were a tumult of colour, but inside the house it was cool and quiet with all the hush of mid-afternoon. The clock in the living room marked the serenity of time. It was a French clock, manifestly so. It stood on an elaborate bronze base and around its face curved garlands of white porcelain roses. Suddenly it whirred and chimed and three silvery notes spilled into the silence.

Adrienne looked up in agitation from her armchair. She got up from her chair and walked to the long mullioned windows. She was determined to remain calm, determined, so much so that her head ached with the effort. Perhaps, she thought, the view would steady her. It looked quite blissful. Summer heat shimmered like tinsel across the line of her vision. Outside the window a lovely eddying breeze blew up, setting the garden in motion. Adrienne gazed in absorption, conscious of the nervous thud of her heartbeat. A yellow leaf came adrift from its fellows, touching down on a shiny black lizard which darted protestingly into the sun-baked pebbles.

For a full minute Adrienne lost track of reality. The world would stand still if she so chose. She felt as light as the leaf, as soft as the sounds from the garden. No problems existed. Then, powerfully, reality reasserted itself. What on earth could be keeping the man? she wondered. Grant Manning might be conspicuous among the landed élite, but an hour was long enough to wait for an interview. Adrienne glanced down at her watch on pure reflex. It was new and rather elegant. It also aroused a considerable reaction, not altogether in keeping with the time. She looked away hurriedly from Linda's parting guilt offering. It made her feel giddy. She thought of Linda, dear Linda, the other Mrs. Brent, her father's second choice – Linda, who was the real reason why Adrienne was now at Saranga. The heart of the matter, Adrienne knew, was her resemblance to her mother. Linda didn't care for any reminders of Madeleine about the house. Not that anyone would blame her. She had had to contend with the beautiful, socially prominent first Mrs. Brent for years before actually replacing her.

Linda had been a long-time employee of the Brent Engineering Firm, starting as a young never sweet thing in the typing pool. From the very first week her possessive young gaze had been filled with her handsome employer and she had never outgrown it, though she was always astute enough to conceal from her colleagues her jealous dislike of his wife. Life hadn't handed Linda any prizes, as she frequently maintained during the tea break. Some women had it all ways – looks, position, a handsome husband, a beautiful child and a well-behaved one too – that was Adrienne, and there she herself was slaving away at a dull desk all day. Many had been the nights when Linda had sat, stultified, at home. No one quite seemed to know why, because she was extremely attractive. It took a slighted and understandably sour admirer from the workshops to hit the nail on the head with professional accuracy. Linda was perversely content with being discontent. Nevertheless she was as stunned as everyone else when Madeleine Brent failed to recover from a relatively minor operation. After two days of near shock, Linda had seen her opportunity. And what an opportunity! It had the blue flame aura of daydreams. Not that it had been easy – far from it. It took four years of unobtrusively smart moves and undemanding togetherness before John Brent finally got round to proposing marriage. Even then she had not felt entirely secure until the actual twenty-minute ceremony was over.

But, with the marriage a *fait accompli*, the façade had fallen. After the intervening years of unfailing sweetness, Adrienne found herself up against a hard core of antagonism, all the more unsettling because it kept shifting. It did her adolescent perceptiveness great credit that she was not unduly disturbed. One female rarely fools another.

On the other hand, her father was, or appeared to be. Though you had to hand it to Linda – when all three of them were together she was something to see; a study in easy camaraderie; they were really like sisters, only they loathed one another.

Not that Linda got off scot-free. As Adrienne got older it became apparent that the house would not hold the two of them. Her stepdaughter was what was known as 'spirited', not that she cared for the trait herself, and she could be alarmingly direct. It was a disconcerting situation, especially when one tried to present a united front at parties. Altogether it had seemed like a godsend when the opportunity of working at Saranga had presented itself. Not only was Saranga one of the richest grazing properties in the country, but it was well over four hundred miles away as well.

Adrienne's soft mouth curved ironically when she thought of that last week at home. Linda had been more affable than the situation demanded; even insisting on a shopping spree to buy suitable clothes for the trip. It seemed she couldn't wait to start. Adrienne hadn't minded the shopping spree. After all, it was her father who was paying, but she did mind Linda's tagging along, and buying along, for that matter. Who was going on the trip anyway?

Her father, man-like, wore blinkers. At first indignant at the idea of his only daughter leaving home, he finally gave way under the two women's seeming enthusiasm. Trust Linda, thought Adrienne, to make it appear that Adrienne was anxious to spread her wings. So she was, but she didn't care to be kicked out of the nest, and that was what it amounted to.

"Poor miserable me," she thought again. But what was the use of dwelling on it? She had come out here for the classic escape. Adrienne pressed her nose against the window pane. "Nothing will diminish my spirit – nothing!" The glass briefly clouded. "Good gracious, there must be at least a hundred feet of decorative ironwork out there!" Saranga boasted a beautiful old homestead, all colonial elegance of white cast-iron lace and mellow sandstone. It wasn't difficult to be impressed. The run-in from the depot had been thrilling and for all her tension she had enjoyed it. Miles and miles of open country, summer charged and fragrant, seemed to stretch on for ever before they came to the soaring beauty of the homestead's entrance. Adrienne had not been prepared for it. Six jacarandas flanked the drive and they were in blossom; incredibly frail and beautiful blossom.

There was a drift of breeze and the great trees swayed in their feathery foliage. Adrienne gazed upwards and lost herself in their mysterious density. The ground was deep with purple blue bells and the air wonderfully stifling. Her senses stirred with the impact. The long driveway curved away gently to the right, allowing the first glimpse of the homestead, vast and white through the low-hanging foliage. Everywhere was the scent of musky, slow-drifting

8

blossoms, emanating from the dense green shadows. In front of the house in the centre of the circular driveway stood a magnificent Poinciana Regis. Its flamboyant blooming seemed a miracle this far south of the tropics. Tier upon tier of scarlet spray loaded its branches, lending the white house a postcard perfection.

The driver from the station, a bow-legged giant called Fred, had been predictably taciturn, but Mrs. Ford, the housekeeper of indeterminate age, who had not exactly greeted her at the front door, had been something of a surprise. She wasn't exactly Mrs. Danvers, but she wasn't Mrs. Mopp either. From previous experience Adrienne had thought housekeepers to be a little on the chatty side. This lady was anything but, for which Adrienne was rather thankful. She had merely shown Adrienne into a breathtaking living room and returned some minutes later with a delicious afternoon tea. It more than made up for her personal shortcomings. But that had been well over an hour ago.

Adrienne had had more than enough time to admire the beautiful Waterford chandelier over her head and its pair in the dining room which she could just see into. She later found out they were bought at a Dublin auction. Her eyes lingered lovingly on the collection of ivory carvings and figurines in the ornamental glass case by the wall. Her mother had owned just such a collection and her father had inexplicably sold it.

She would never get over it. Even as a child her mother had allowed her to handle the precious and intricate carvings as a special privilege and to accustom her to appreciating beautiful things.

Everyone knew there was money at Saranga, but there was also exquisite taste. The interior decoration was reminiscent of homes she had seen on the Continent, but was rather surprising for the Australian out-back – or was it? These people were wealthy enough to have the best of both worlds. One thing was certain – they had a penchant for antiques. Her unseeing gaze settled on some early Italian flower paintings. What could be keeping the master of Saranga? She was beginning to feel quite ill and aimless.

Almost immediately there was a slight commotion in the hall and the sound of a man's voice, attractive and decisive. Adrienne's heart gave one awful anticipatory bump and at that moment a tall, deeply tanned man in his early thirties came through the swinging glass doors.

He looked arrogant and clever and a man to contend with. Her fascinated gaze veered away from the arresting light eyes, skidded over the high cheekbones, skipped the mouth and came to rest on the cleft in his chin. He took an age to speak.

"Good afternoon, Miss Brent. I'm sorry you've been kept waiting."

He didn't sound in the least sorry, but inclined his head for her to be seated, remaining standing just to be formidable, Adrienne supposed. She felt at a definite disadvantage, so she characteristically launched into speech. Surprise was the essence of attack, wasn't it? "Perhaps you'll take pity on me, Mr. Manning, and tell me what you're thinking?" she demanded briskly. She watched him light a cigarette and inhale deeply.

"You're remarkably unlike my idea of a secretary, Miss Brent, though I might not be the best one to judge. Bert Parker was no oil painting." Bert Parker, she thought, must be her predecessor – secretary, jackaroo, horse-breaker. Adrienne's head came up aggressively, sensing rejection. Dark eyes sparkled at him in unwilling admiration and resentment.

His glance assumed a becoming candour.

"Please don't misunderstand me, Miss Brent. I'm all for decorative young women, even highly-strung ones, as you appear to be, but I don't know that I can afford the luxury of having one in the office. I've a ton of work to get through."

Adrienne gasped. unable to credit his statement. These weren't Victorian times; she didn't have to beg for the position. She rose to her feet with a slightly hysterical flourish.

"Sex rears its ugly head, I take it – or typical outback thinking, Mr. Manning. I wouldn't raise a yawn in the city, I assure you." She smoothed on her short white gloves in a temper, good sense forgotten. "I need hardly say you're something of a disappointment to me, too."

There was an expressive little silence and Adrienne felt the first tremor of alarm. She was burning her boats too rapidly. She felt compelled to look up, only to find him amused.

"My dear Miss Brent, my very dear Miss Brent," he exaggerated sardonically, "I fear I've offended you with my quaint country ways. But surely you do yourself an injustice. A beautiful woman can still topple a man's peace of mind; even in Sydney. I do commute occasionally."

Adrienne bit on her lip, fast losing her poise. "I can only say your natural caution doesn't apply in this case, Mr. Manning. I'm not a beautiful woman, merely a working girl."

Light eyes flinted mockingly. "That's all too easily remedied, Miss Brent."

Adrienne felt faintly shocked! Was he trying to reduce her to a gauche girl? "I feel the conversation is vaguely improper, Mr. Manning," she managed, sounding hopelessly prim.

One black eyebrow shot up. "My dear girl, if it is, you started it."

Adrienne fought for finesse against his easy, teasing manner.

"It so happens, Miss Brent . . ." He was overdoing that Miss Brent, she thought a shade irritably. His gaze sharpened, reading hers accurately. "It so happens, my dear, I'm a typical outback man, busy and with a great deal of paper work I could quite happily relegate." His glance held the sheen of sarcasm. "But only if you could overlook your initial disappointment. In any case I haven't the time or patience to wait for your possible replacement," he finished up. She found him tactless. "You can type, Miss Brent?" he pushed on.

Adrienne fought for finesse against his easy, teasing opportunity to impress you, Mr. Manning," she murmured silkily.

His teeth showed very white against his tan. Grant was suddenly offhand. "I'll be out for the rest of the day. Ask Mrs. Ford if there's anything you need. She'll look after you until my aunt returns." At the door he turned casually. "By the way, Miss Brent, as a concession to your countrified employer, would you tie back your hair during working hours at least. I find it very distracting." Adrienne put up a hand to her mahogany hair, but he was gone.

CHAPTER TWO

ADRIENNE woke next morning to the sound of a kookaburra in the blue gum at the far corner of the verandah. She stretched her arms above her head, enjoying the morning and her sense of well-being. The unmistakable fragrance of jasmine wafted in great puffs through the open french windows which gave on to the verandah, and the sun through the creepers dappled the beautiful cedar furnishings of her room. It was heavenly!

Her accommodation left nothing to be desired by the most exacting guest, let alone employee. She had, in fact, a unit to herself, bedroom, bathroom and adjoining sitting room. The bathroom was a recent conversion from a huge walk-in wardrobe, as eye-catching as it was functional. Burmese gold tiles glimmered softly from the walls, floor and side of the small square bath set into a shower recess. Adrienne stood for a good ten minutes admiring the fibre-glass shower screen inset with waving reeds, shells and sand to resemble the sea bed. In the sliding glass panels backing the vanity counter were several beautifully shaped jars in aquamarine glass to match the bath and vanity basin. Obviously the Mannings meant her to be happy in her surroundings. Mrs. Ford had unbent slightly when she had given Adrienne a pleasantly heavy-handed tour around the homestead the previous afternoon; perhaps she too had been suspicious of decorative young women.

It appeared that Mrs. Manning, the lady of the house, and unquestionably the first lady of the community, was expected back from a Country Women's Conference within a few days.

Adrienne wondered what she would make of her. She sounded almost as formidable as her nephew. But let the future take care of itself. Adrienne got up at once, did a few swinging exercises to wake herself completely, and turned on the shower. It was a pleasure to have it at the bottom of the ocean. A little later, bathed, dressed and with her hair in a soft French pleat, she went down to the breakfast room. Everything had been set on the sideboard, but Adrienne found she was too keyed up to have more than coffee and a freshly baked roll. Mrs. Ford prided herself on her cooking and with reason. Last night's dinner had been superb. Adrienne had enjoyed it all the more because she had it alone – the Master of Saranga was apparently out to dinner. After her third cup of coffee, Adrienne was wondering what to do next when Grant Manning came into the room, looking very much like *Vogue*'s idea of the man of the land in riding clothes. The cool grey eyes flickered over her, taking in every detail of her appearance, the buttercup silk shirt and colour-matched skirt, the neat little head, the hair-style drawing attention to its beautiful bone structure. He was anything but unobservant of a woman's appearance.

"You look very . . . composed, Miss Brent. I was going to say businesslike, but I see the word doesn't suit you," he murmured with gentle mockery.

What on earth was he talking about? – not "business-like", she thought. She had a diploma to prove it.

"Well, you'd better come along to the office before I change my mind," he remarked cryptically, and turned towards the door. Adrienne got up from the table, pushed in her chair quickly and followed him through the long cool passageway, past several large rooms, and out to the west wing of the house.

His office was enormous, filled with books and files, accounts records, journals, pastoral companies' periodicals, and what seemed like mountains of opened and unopened correspondence. Adrienne stood aghast, and he went to the executive desk and began leafing through the unopened mail. His manner was preoccupied and Adrienne had the rather uncomfortable feeling that he had forgotten her existence. With a sudden movement he looked up and his glance was a little satirical.

"Think you can cope?" he enquired crisply. "The mail has to be sorted. You'll probably be able to draft a reply to the routine stuff. Others you'll know to leave for me. The main thing is to get the pile down." He gestured towards the avalanche and Adrienne straightened her shoulders and walked into the room.

"I should be able to manage, Mr Manning." She sounded quite cool, but added a few inner amendments.

"Good girl, then go to it while I beat a retreat." He nodded briefly and went out, his footsteps echoing along the passageway. When they had receded Adrienne went around to the table, cleared adequate space, and settled down to sort things out.

Good grief, what the man had to cope with! Queries from firms and organisations, requests, and what requests, from various charities and institutions, petitions for his presence at pastoral meetings, seemingly all over the country, articles for monthly periodicals for a thousand and one things Adrienne would have supposed to be outside his range of concern.

She arranged the letters according to what she could handle and put paper into the machine. By lunchtime she had made considerable headway and felt pleasantly flushed with achievement. So engrossed was she that Adrienne failed to notice Mrs. Ford standing at the doorway holding a laden tray. The housekeeper jangled a spoon and Adrienne looked up startled. "I'm afraid I forgot the time, Mrs. Ford. I'm sorry you had to come for me."

"That's all right, my dear, Mr. Manning has a party of businessmen to lunch and he thought you would be happier here."

"Yes, of course," Adrienne murmured, and came to her feet to take the tray. "This looks wonderful, Mrs. Ford," she commented quite truthfully and, looking up, caught a glimmering of approval on the other woman's face.

"You'll have plenty of work if you stay here, my dear."
Mrs. Ford gestured towards the now orderly desk. "This
district revolves around Mr. Grant and he has enough
energy for ten men, but all this paper work ties him
down."

Adrienne nodded in heartfelt agreement and glanced
back over her shoulder. "I can see that it would, Mrs.
Ford, and I'm here to help." Mrs. Ford smiled agreeably
and, realising that she was frittering away precious time,
took herself back along the passageway, her soft shoes
making little noise on the polished floors. Adrienne
returned to the desk, suddenly realising how hungry she
was.

What was here! Chicken, salad, crisp home-made rolls,
curls of butter, coffee black and strong the way she liked
it, and a selection of tiny cakes. Heavens, she thought,
they certainly lived well at Saranga! She would get fat. She
settled comfortably into her chair, switching on the fan as
she did so. It was noon and the sun was swinging into full
power. She could see the heat waves shimmering outside
the window. In another few weeks it would be a scorcher.
Somewhere not far off, she clearly heard Grant Manning's
voice and that of another man's not nearly so decisive. She
decided not to linger over lunch and turned back to the
correspondence. Thank heavens she was used to an elec-
tric typewriter; with so much work to attend to, it
wouldn't do to have to get used to the typewriter as well.
She drafted a few replies in her head and put paper into the
machine – no erasions for Mr. Manning. Some time later
she heard footsteps in the passageway and kept her head
down. Her employer would appreciate that. He rapped
lightly on the doorway and came into the room together
with a fair-haired young man. The newcomer was of middle height with powerful shoulders and a bright engaging
face. His eyes were deep blue and he was looking at
Adrienne much as he would a mirage.

"How's it going?" Grant queried with a faint tinge of

sarcasm, but before Adrienne had an opportunity to reply the newcomer burst out, "Great snakes alive, Gray, if you're not going to, I'll introduce myself."

Grant laughed and rested a lean brown hand on the desk. "Allow me to introduce my cousin, Miss Brent – Christopher Harrington from Careewa – our nearest neighbour."

Christopher bounded in and shook Adrienne's hand with obvious enthusiasm. "Hello, Adrienne," he said, still holding her hand. "Grant told me he had someone for the office, but I never imagined it would be you – I mean I never imagined it would be someone like you. Heck, I'd never coop you in an office!"

Grant's voice cut neatly through the conversation. "Right-oh, Chris, you've made a very good point. Miss Brent is nevertheless here to work . . . and greatly enhance Saranga." He finished with an unexpected quirk to his mouth. Adrienne felt a trifle overwhelmed.

She managed to disengage her hand and spoke to Chris, a smile showing her small perfect teeth. "It's a pleasure to meet you, Mr. Harrington, and a nice break from the filing," she murmured, with a sideways glance at her employer.

Chris threw back his fair head. "Good grief!" he shouted with laughter. "No one, but no one, calls me Mr. Harrington. Chris, Adrienne, Chris," he ordered, "since I'm going to see a lot of you."

Adrienne felt the conversation getting out of hand. She turned back to the desk and started to collect the finished letters. "I have these ready for your signature, Mr. Manning," she said, her voice somewhat subdued. She hoped he wouldn't find anything amiss, especially in front of a third party.

Adrienne smiled at Chris, but felt her nerves tightening with apprehension. After a few minutes Grant straightened up and his grey eyes met hers with sardonic appreciation. "Very good, Miss Brent, very good indeed," he

17

commented. "Sign them for me and put them in the mail bag for the driver." He turned to Chris, one hand on his shoulder, and impelled him towards the door. "Say goodbye to Miss Brent, Chris. It may be some time before you'll be seeing her."

But Chris was an enterprising young man. He swung back to Adrienne. "Do you ride, Adrienne?" he queried, never expecting an answer.

Adrienne shrugged rather helplessly. "I'm afraid I don't, Chris."

"Good grief!" Grant exploded impatiently. "You're out here and you can't ride? I don't believe it!" Adrienne felt the temper rise in her and it showed momentarily in her face. She sparkled a look at him and he finished in an ordinary tone. "Be down at the stables at six tomorrow morning. I presume you've got some kind of gear with you."

"Don't worry, Adrienne," Chris smiled at her. "I'll show you, never fear; there's nothing to it."

Grant's hand came ruthlessly to the back of his cousin's head. "Goodbye now, Miss Brent. Tell Mrs. Ford I'll be at Careewa for the rest of the day." Chris disappeared with a cheerful wave of his hand. Evidently he was used to his autocratic cousin.

Adrienne leaned back in her chair and let the sun through the tall windows soak over her. It was strong now and slanted over her glossy red head, burnishing the highlights. She closed her eyes, seeing colour pictures of what the morning would bring.

All that night Adrienne hardly slept, but lay for hours watching the moonlight filter through the vines; her mind too active for sleep. Saranga was another world, a rather wonderful world far removed from home and Linda. Chris Harrington was definitely on her side. He for one had no objection to decorative young women. "Decorative" . . . she said the word aloud and decided she disliked it intensely. She had always taken her looks for granted. They were a blessing bestowed on one at birth, though heaven knew anyone could look attractive these days. She went back over her interview with Grant Manning and felt the same awful confusion. She wasn't sure what to make of him; he was much too much for the working girl. Heaven knew what she would do if he ever unleashed the full weight of his charm. "I'd probably disintegrate," she whispered.

Adrienne moved restlessly in the bed and made a determined effort to put Grant Manning out of her mind. Saranga seemed the appropriate place to count sheep. The next thing she remembered was the sound of the alarm, and she catapulted out of bed. In spite of her anxiety for the morning, Adrienne found herself humming as she dressed in a cream silk blouse and tan slacks – she hoped that these would be considered suitable, but they were all that she had anyway. She studied her face in the early morning light and decided that she would do. She was well out into the hallway before she realised that she had not tied back her hair.

The air smelt lemon-fresh and the grass of the drive was thick under her feet. It was very still with the promise of the heat to come. Adrienne was wide awake and ready for anything or almost anything. Grant Manning was beyond her limited experience. She continued on through the trees and saw the stables to her left. There didn't seem to be a sign of life; perhaps he had forgotten her. Adrienne hesitated, not knowing whether to return to the house or wait in the hope that he would turn up. She didn't have to wait for long. There was a crunch of footsteps on the gravel and she recognised his firm tread before turning her head.

Grant came towards her, swinging a riding crop. He looked very much what he was, and Adrienne felt suddenly shy of him. "A punctual woman is above rubies, or something like that, Miss Brent." He came closer and the

19

smooth grey glance slid over her attire. "Those slacks will be too tight in the leg, but they'll do until we get you some gear from the town." He studied her delicately flushed young face and his voice was a little dry. "Not nervous, I hope?"

Adrienne's tongue flicked her pink underlip, but she replied with spirit. "Whatever made you think that, Mr. Manning? I've often intended taking lessons; this will be as good a time as any."

Grant moved past her to the stables and came out leading a chestnut mare. Her sides looked sleek and she was swishing her tail. At the sight of Adrienne she lifted her head and her ears pricked forward. Her eyes were large and dark and only mildly curious, and Adrienne felt a little happier. With Grant Manning she almost expected a fractious yearling.

"This is Gemma," he said. "She's quiet and gentle, so there's no need to be afraid."

Evidently he had ignored her brave words. The mare flicked her tail and reached out an enquiring muzzle at the girl. Adrienne put her hand up and caressed the soft muzzle and the mare breathed lovingly down the front of her blouse. Adrienne saw the flash of amusement in Grant's eyes and then he leaned over and gently handed off the mare.

"She seems to like you," he laughed, "so that will make it easier. Come over here." Adrienne followed. For the next hour she was shown how to mount, dismount, hold the reins, place her feet in the stirrups and adjust the girth. It would take time to become accustomed to the walk, feel and movement of a horse beneath her.

Grant persisted until the rhythm of the trot was fairly mastered. Then he called it a day. Surprisingly enough he was a good teacher, patient and methodical. From the unusual atmosphere of accord between them, Adrienne felt that she was acquitting herself reasonably well, and a feeling of exhileration shot through her. At the end of the lesson, Grant helped her dismount and, over-confident, her foot caught in the stirrup and she half fell into his upstretched arms. For an endless moment she lay within the circle of his arms and then she was set briskly on her feet. His voice in her ear was soft and derisive. "That was an unorthodox descent from a horse, Miss Brent."

Adrienne gave a shaken little laugh and the dark eyes she raised to his held more than a little agitation in their velvet depths. The breeze lifted the collar of her blouse and fanned out her hair. Seemingly without conscious volition his hand came out and tucked back a stray lock. Then it dropped abruptly and he turned back to the mare. Gemma jerked up her head and the bit jangled.

"Get some riding in every day. I'll get someone to watch you. We'll get some clothes for you when my aunt returns. Cut along now for breakfast." Adrienne felt she'd been well and truly dismissed, so she turned and made her way slowly back along the drive . . .

For the rest of the week Adrienne saw nothing of her employer and she was glad of the respite from his disturbing presence. It was impossible to be indifferent to him and it was equally impossible to be at ease with him. Altogether, she considered, the less she saw of him the better. She attended to the filing which had been more or less kept up to date and typed up several articles which he had written for periodicals. The sun had almost gone down and the office was darkening before she was finished. There was a soft fall of footsteps along the passageway and the next minute Mrs. Ford appeared at the open doorway.

"Good heavens, dear, surely you're not working in this bad light? She advanced into the room and switched on the main light.

Adrienne blinked and put her hands up to her eyes. "I was too busy to stop, but I'm finished now, thank goodness." She bent over and retrieved the typewriter cover from the floor.

21

Mrs. Ford watched her fit it over the machine, then she remarked informatively, "Mrs. Manning will be back this evening. She'll be at home for dinner, so I thought you might like to change into a pretty dress."

Adrienne got up from the desk and smiled warmly. "Yes, I would, Mrs. Ford. Thank you for coming along to tell me. Mrs. Manning would be Mr. Manning's aunt on his father's side, of course."

"That's right, dear. It still grieves me to say it, but Mr. Grant's father and his uncle were killed when the Cessna came down in the mountains. Saranga has its own private plane and air-strip, you know. Grant's uncle was piloting the plane. It was a shocking day in these parts, I can tell you. That was fourteen years ago and Mrs. Manning has lived here ever since. She makes a trip overseas every few years, but she always returns to Saranga. You'll find her a little aloof at first, but she's a fine woman and has devoted her life to the community since her husband died." Mrs. Ford sighed, her mind obviously going back over the years.

Adrienne crossed through to her room and made a quick run through her clothes. Mrs. Ford had said "something pretty", but how pretty could she go? After all, she wasn't a guest. Her hand flicked along the row and came to rest on a black shift. It was round-necked, sleeveless and trimmed with tiny gold buttons. Yes, this was suitable. She always felt happy and comfortable in it. Adrienne had a quick shower, made up her face carefully, dressed her hair in a French pleat and slipped into the dress. It lightly skimmed her slight body and displayed her golden limbs to advantage. She clipped on gold leaf earrings, adjusted the strap of her gold sandals and used just a touch of Miss Dior on her wrists and throat. It was just on six o'clock as she walked into the living room.

There were voices coming from the room and Adrienne felt a trifle nervous. If Mrs. Manning was against her that would take care of everything. She reached the doorway

22

and hesitated uncertainly. The room seemed to be full of people and they turned towards her standing like a ballerina in the wings. Grant Manning detached himself from the group and came over to her, his manner smooth and charming. He took hold of her arm drawing her into the room.

"Adrienne, I'd like you to meet my aunt, Mrs. Manning," his arm tightening as she started at the use of her Christian name. He was unpredictable! Mrs. Manning remained seated, but put out one very bejewelled hand, smiling pleasantly.

"How do you do, my dear. Grant told me about you. I must say, though, I never expected someone so lovely. You could be a model."

Adrienne flushed at the intended compliment and took hold of the extended hand. Why should she want to be a model, for heaven's sake? She disliked being stared at. Mrs. Manning was about fifty and still a beauty. She looked anything but a countrywoman with her fine clear skin, expertly tinted, and her expensive clothes. Her manner was only faintly pampered and her hair was sculptured silver. Adrienne smiled into the larkspur blue eyes and found the smile returned.

Grant turned her slightly and she found herself being introduced to a tall, elegant, fair girl who regarded her with close on dislike, and not a quite effeminate young man, obviously her brother, who smiled rather intimately. "Vera and Brian Sterling from Carnarvon Station."

"I've made an enemy there," Adrienne thought, as she registered the stony look in the other girl's eyes. Then she saw Vera's eyes following Grant around the room and she thought, "How stupid – trespassers will be shot after one warning, and I've had it. Well, she need have no fear of any competition from me." Her mouth tilted.

"Get Adrienne a sherry, Grant dear." Mrs. Manning broke into her thoughts. "And then we can go into dinner."

Grant looked at Adrienne, a gleam of sardonic mockery in his eyes. "Sweet or dry, Adrienne? Or topped up with ginger ale?"

"Dry, thank you, Grant," she answered coolly, and had the satisfaction of seeing one black eyebrow shoot up. For an instant there was a look on his face that she could not quite read, then he came over to her and handed her the sherry, gleaming topaz in a crystal glass. Carefully Adrienne took it, feigning interest in its scintillations.

"Does Miss Brent address you by your Christian name, Grant?" Vera queried incredulously.

Grant crushed out his cigarette and before he could reply his aunt broke in. "What else, dear girl?" Her delicate eyebrows were arching and her tone was one of slight rebuke. "After all, this isn't the usual type of position, and Adrienne is living in the house."

Adrienne felt her cheeks grow hot with embarrassment and regretted whatever impulse she had had that made her call her employer Grant. They were all rather relieved when Mrs. Ford came to the door to announce that dinner was ready.

As it turned out, the meal, although delicious, was anything but harmonious. Vera sat in an aggressive silence while her brother's eyes flickered continually over Adrienne, as though he was trying to make up his mind about something. Grant, though he indulged in the usual pleasantries, seemed preoccupied, and it was only Mrs. Manning's presence that saved the day. Adrienne was grateful to her for steering what conversation there was into fairly normal channels. Vera's remark in the dining room had somehow created a tension where there should not have been one, and Adrienne wished for the meal to end so that she could escape to the privacy of her rooms. She waited until coffee was served and excused herself on the pretext of having to write home. Mrs. Manning waved a patrician hand and invited her to a long chat the next day.

Out in the hallway she could hear the other girl's voice, affected but not unpleasant. "Well, I do think she's rather forward, and there's no need for her to be so . . . dressy." Adrienne heard no more but fled to her room, anger beating in her temples. What a ghastly girl with a manner to match. "Dressy!" The word reverberated in her head. She hoped she wouldn't be seeing much of the Sterlings. She hated them both!

In the chaste light of early morning Adrienne went down to the stables. Gemma seemed to be waiting for her and she made the most of her hour. There were a few hands about with nice easy manners and plenty of advice. Further on, past the stables, was the sound of much activity and Adrienne would have liked to investigate. As yet, she hadn't seen around the property except the long drive from the bus depot. She was looking forward to being shown over it and hoped that Grant would find the time to do so, although wondering how long it would take to see over a hundred and thirty thousand acres in the heart of the sheep country, famous for its aristocratic rams and their prize fat lambs. It wasn't surprising that Grant also ran an excellent stud, rapidly coming to the forefront in bloodstock breeding. He really was the most amazing man, running a small world with remarkable efficiency.

Adrienne wondered what he thought of Vera Sterling. She had the looks of a rather classy racehorse herself and was in all probability a splendid horsewoman. She should be anyway, Adrienne thought rather waspishly, with that head start. Vera's brother, although he tried to be pleasant, gave the impression of not having much character, though Grant's blazing presence would dim any man's impact.

Adrienne was just turning into the drive when she saw Grant and Vera both in riding attire come down the steps of the homestead. What a moment to pick! Adrienne waved a greeting, saw Grant lift a hand in salute, while his companion looked determinedly ahead. Adrienne cut down the side of the house, thinking her own thoughts.

After breakfast Adrienne was told that Mrs. Manning would like to see her in her study, so she went through to the east wing of the house and knocked on the door. She heard Mrs. Manning call "Come in" and turned the knob, pausing at the open doorway.

It was a beautiful sitting room-study, furnished in the grand manner, as befitting its owner. Mrs. Manning got to her feet and came towards her with a great deal of charm in her smile. "Come in, dear, and I can find out a little about you. We didn't have much opportunity to talk last night." She gestured to an armchair upholstered in mauve and gold striped silk and returned to her seat behind the desk. She smiled pleasantly at Adrienne and leaned back before going on. She looked a woman in entire control of herself and one who had important things to attend to. Adrienne remembered Mrs. Ford saying that she was very active in community affairs.

"I know you're here to help Grant, Adrienne, and heaven knows he needs it, but I wonder if you could spare me some time too whenever you're not busy with Grant's affairs. I'm frantically busy myself at different times and I would be very grateful for your assistance whenever I can get it." She paused for a moment and added reassuringly, "It's quite all right with Grant, if you're wondering about it."

Adrienne smiled. "I'd be glad to, Mrs. Manning."

"Good. Dear Grant tells me you're very competent."

Adrienne felt a quiver along her nerves. So he did find her competent as well as decorative! That was something from Mrs. Manning.

Mrs. Manning was speaking, her voice firm and businesslike. "You know, Adrienne, we're adding a maternity ward to the local hospital. At the moment our mothers have to travel into Mitchell, a not very satisfactory arrangement. You can well imagine the amount of

26

work that is involved with a programme like that, and most of it falls on me. Not that I mind. It gives me something constructive to do."

She turned her head slightly until her gaze rested on the poinsettia flaming outside the window. It seemed her thoughts were very far away. Adrienne guessed that life in a sense had been hard on Mrs. Manning, tragically widowed as she had been early in life. Perhaps that was one reason for all her commitments. The silver head came back to Adrienne. "There'll be a women's committee meeting in town on Wednesday. I shall be chairing it and I want you to come in with me to take the minutes, if you would. We can get you some riding gear at the same time."

Adrienne felt there was little that Grant had failed to mention to his aunt. They both turned at a tap on the door. After a momentary pause Mrs. Ford came in, bringing with her the delicious fragrance of coffee and hot buttered scones.

"You're too good to us," Mrs. Manning said as Adrienne got up and pulled forward an occasional table. "I've missed all your little attentions since I've been away."

Mrs. Ford smiled sedately, taking the compliment in her stride. She was used to Mrs. Manning's somewhat studied graciousness, none the less pleasant for all that. "Will Mr. Grant and Miss Sterling be in to lunch?"

"No, Mrs. Ford, I should have mentioned it, but it just slipped my mind. I think we can expect them when we see them," she added with a tiny laugh.

Mrs. Ford stood there unsmiling, her hands absently smoothing the folds of her apron, then she inclined her head and opened the door, shutting it quietly behind her.

"Grant and Vera have been friends since they were children," Mrs. Manning explained somewhat unnecessarily. "Although Grant is five years older, of course they have a great deal in common." Her voice was light and conversational, but Adrienne thought she detected an undertone – or was it a warning? Adrienne remained silent, not knowing what she was expected to say, if anything, then Mrs. Manning briskly changed the subject and began to talk to Adrienne of herself. Her manner was anything but inquisitive, but all the same Adrienne felt that there was very little Mrs. Manning had not found out, short of her blood group, in the most charming way possible. One thing which was certain was her very real affection for her nephew, even if he was a nephew by marriage only.

The two women lingered over their morning coffee and then Adrienne collected the tray and returned it to the kitchen before crossing to the office to attend to the morning's mail. One of the station hands went into the town each morning and always came back with a load. Adrienne threw open the windows, breathed in the lovely summer smell and then went to work. It was as well that she was a girl of intelligence and initiative, because the position required both qualities. It was obvious that Grant Manning had spent many hours at his desk, and Adrienne guessed that these were long night hours as he was on the go from early morning until dinnertime with the outdoors and affairs of the station.

She sorted out what she could deal with herself, what obviously needed Grant's attention, and a creditable pile of correspondence addressed to Mrs. Manning. It was some hours later when she heard a light tread on the polished floors and, looking up, she saw Vera Sterling lounging rather insolently in the doorway.

"I heard you making an impressive show of typing," Vera said pointedly. "I suppose you thought I was Grant."

"Hardly," Adrienne replied sarcastically. "I don't imagine he goes tippy-toeing around the passageway, he has a different tread altogether, as you would imagine."

"Really!" the other girl countered, taken aback. "You haven't been here long enough to recognise Grant's tread, or anyone else's for that matter."

Adrienne clicked her tongue. She didn't wish to pursue such an inane line of argument. Vera pulled forward a chair, lounged back in it and drew a packet of cigarettes from the pocket of her jodhpurs. She was beautifully got up and looked extremely well in her riding costume. Adrienne guessed that it would be the look that would suit her best. She lit her cigarette and blew out a great puff of smoke, deliberately giving such an impression of unguarded animosity that Adrienne was a little startled at the extent of the other girl's dislike. She couldn't imagine herself getting that worked up in similar circumstances, but then you never knew. She laughed at the idea and Vera's eyes narrowed in surprised dislike.

"I just thought I'd come along and give you a few words of advice that might save you a lot of embarrassment," Vera remarked tersely. "Don't make the mistake of imagining yourself one of the family! You're by no means indispensable to Grant, and I know he's in two minds about you. Being a man of course he would hesitate to mention it. I thought I would do him a favour. After all," she added, "we're very close."

Adrienne watched her fastidiously flick a few grains of ash from her knee and made a considerable effort to control herself. She knew quite well that Grant wouldn't hesitate to mention anything if he chose to do so, and she was well aware of the malice behind Vera's remarks.

"How good of you to think of me, Miss Sterling," she said, her voice warm and grateful. "I'll endeavour to take your words to heart." She kept her eyes down lest they mirrored her mood too faithfully, while her features remained cool and composed. After a moment, Adrienne felt able to look up. "I wonder if you will excuse me, Miss Sterling. I have some letters to take through to Mrs. Manning."

"I'll take them," the other girl said, stretching out an imperious hand.

"Thank you for offering," Adrienne replied, retaining

29

the letters. "Mrs. Manning may like me to attend to some of the routine ones for her." She crossed round the desk and, nodding pleasantly to the fair girl in the chair, walked out of the room.

Vera waited until Adrienne had gone, then she got up and walked round the desk. It appeared the girl could type and very well too. Heavens, what a long memorandum! Just long enough . . . she flicked her ash viciously on the typewritten page, watched it burn a hole in the paper, then strolled casually out of the room.

Mrs. Manning and Adrienne dined alone that evening, and a very pleasant occasion it turned out to be. Adrienne found the older woman to be an easy and interesting conversationalist, well-read and knowledgeable. To their mutual satisfaction the two women found they had a great deal in common, including a deep love of music. When Adrienne mentioned that she was a Conservatorium-trained pianist, Mrs. Manning was genuinely delighted.

"My dear, I have a beautiful Bechstein grand stored in Sydney. I used to play myself, you know, not really well as I somehow know you do, but adequately. I'll have it sent out. It will be good for both of us."

Adrienne felt the quick tears prick her eyes. Leaving her own beautiful piano behind had been just one of the sacrifices she had had to make. Now the prospect of having another was almost too much for her.

They lingered over coffee and when the two women parted company for the night, each felt a small glow of pleasure in the other's company.

Adrienne was just laying her things out for the night when there was a knock on the door. She opened it and found Grant on the threshold. He was impeccably dressed in a light grey lounge suit with a brown silk tie. His chiselled dark features were thrown into vivid relief against his snowy linen. He looked tall and lean and intensely virile. He had no time for preliminaries, it seemed. "Come down to the office, Adrienne, like a good girl," he said crisply. "I've something I want you to do for me."

Adrienne followed him through the house and found the west wing ablaze with lights. Evidently he had been there before her. He stood back for her to precede him into the office, then crossed to the filing cabinet. "Thank goodness that's up to date," he said forcibly. He pulled out a neatly labelled folder and turned back to her.

"Sit down." He waved an arm imperiously, his cuff links catching the light. She did so, then he continued briefly. "Going on some information I received today I want to close a deal with Wilks Ferguson. I have some Americans coming tomorrow to look at one of my stallions, so I'll be tied up with them all day. We'll get a few pertinent letters off tonight so they'll be ready for the mail in the morning. Could you get these down?" he demanded briskly.

"I could put them straight into the machine if you like . . ."

"Right, let's get going."

Grant dictated for the next half hour without a break, then broke off abruptly, crushing out his half smoked cigarette. "I think we'll have some coffee, don't you? Whatever it is they serve at the hotel, it's frightful."

Adrienne concluded, incorrectly as it happened, that he must have dined there with Vera. "I'll make some," she offered, and rose quickly to her feet – a little too quickly. She stretched gingerly and arched her throat to relieve the tension on her neck muscles. When her glance came back to him she found the grey eyes glittering half with amusement and half with – was it speculation?

She gave him a sudden sweet smile and almost immediately the atmosphere changed. A silence stretched between them and Adrienne looked away from the incongruity of his light eyes and spoke quickly to cover her momentary confusion. "Strong and black, is that right?"

"Yes," he conceded smoothly. "I'll look through these while you make it."

Adrienne walked back along the passageway and snapped on the kitchen light. Mrs. Ford had retired for the night, but her domain was spotless. She certainly had a dream kitchen to work in . . . double ovens set into the wall, and an island unit of hotplates, plenty of cupboards of white and gold specked laminate outlined in gold, and a display alcove holding lovely pieces of porcelain and recipe books.

Adrienne walked into the huge, well-stocked pantry and ran her eye along the canisters. She reached down a tin of caramel and mocha and took a few deep breaths to steady herself. Fancy being so susceptible to Grant's particular brand of masculinity! Surely she had imagined that moment of magnetism between them? Adrienne shrugged it off and consoled herself with the thought that there wouldn't be many women immune to him. While the coffee was perking, she leant back against the cupboard and closed her eyes.

"Don't doze off, Miss Brent, it's coffee time," he mocked from the open doorway, and Adrienne started visibly. His eyes narrowed, noting the soft colour which sprang to her cheeks, then he crossed to a wall cupboard and took down cups and saucers.

Adrienne managed a cool little laugh, her self-possession returning. "Actually I was resting my eyes. I always find fluorescent lighting a strain."

His mouth twitched and he murmured, "What a recovery!"

Adrienne was glad the coffee indicator light came on, for it gave her something to do. She poured the coffee, which smelt marvellous and tasted almost as good, and went back into the pantry for some chocolate biscuits. She was just coming back with them when a high brittle voice from the doorway enquired acidly. "Is this a private party or is anyone invited?"

They both turned their heads and Vera swished into the kitchen, wearing a gorgeous jade dressing gown. It was of quilted satin and gleamed alluringly under the light, though the vee of the neckline plunged rather alarmingly. Her eyes had caught a little of its colour, but it seemed to Adrienne that Vera was pale under her tan.

"I couldn't call coffee a party, Vera, but you're certainly invited," Grant answered smoothly. He pulled out a chair and saw her seated.

Adrienne brought over another cup and Vera remarked stiltedly, "Cream for me, Miss Brent." Adrienne took cream from the refrigerator and went to pour it into a jug. "I have it whipped, thank you," the other girl said sharply.

Adrienne started to count to ten when Grant broke in easily. "There doesn't appear to be any, Vera. Won't the other do?"

"It will have to, darling, won't it?" she shrugged.

Adrienne got up, balancing her cup carefully. "If you'll just excuse me," she said, "I'll type the envelopes for those letters," and went out without a backward glance. What an unbearable beast of a girl! she thought. Dislike between them was mutual.

About fifteen minutes later, Grant came through to the office, his expression unreadable. "It's just on ten," he said, flicking back the cuff of his jacket. "Time we called it a day. Did you get through here?"

Adrienne nodded, her throat a little tight. "Yes, everything's attended to."

"Good girl," he said, his tone impersonal. "Come on now, and I'll turn off the light."

Adrienne covered the typewriter and came around the desk to him. He took the letters from her, looked through them and waited until she had crossed to the doorway. The light flickered off and Adrienne was intensely aware of him standing near to her in the dark. Her heart was beating rather fast and she felt irritated with herself for

33

finding him so attractive. His hand came out and closed on the soft skin of her arm as he propelled her out into the hallway. She withdrew slightly from his touch and he dropped his hand immediately. Had he guessed her coolness was only a pretence and warm blood pulsed beneath his hand?

"You go along," he ordered off-handedly. "I'll switch off here." Adrienne gave him a polite goodnight, her long lashes veiling her eyes, and went quickly to her room.

CHAPTER THREE

THE next morning Adrienne saw Grant briefly as she went into breakfast. He was dressed for the outdoors and looked like a man in a hurry. "Have the morning off," he called, breaking his stride to the front door. "That's an order."

Adrienne managed a fairly steady "Thank you" and went into the dining room. It was empty, but presently Mrs. Manning came in, immaculate in ice-blue linen. Adrienne wondered how she kept her hair so beautifully, miles away from the fashionable salons. She stood up and the older woman waved her back into her chair.

Mrs. Manning crossed to the sideboard, helped herself to piping hot scrambled eggs from under a covered warming dish, and came back to the table. "Sleep well, Adrienne?"

"Yes, I did, thank you, Mrs. Manning. I love my rooms, and the smell of honeysuckle and jasmine wafting in is sheer heaven."

"Yes, it's wonderfully heady, isn't it? I love it too."

She spread a slice of toast thinly with butter, scrupulously scraped it all off, and looked up imploringly. "Did you see my mail, dear? Could you be an angel and find some time for me today?"

"Why not this morning?" Adrienne offered. She would be hard put to fill in the morning anyway.

"Grant doesn't want you?" Mrs. Manning queried on a rising inflection.

"Not this morning," Adrienne answered quite truthfully.

Mrs. Manning breathed a sigh of relief. "How fortunate, I have such a lot to catch up on. Come along about ten, I should have things sorted out by then."

They finished breakfast in an amicable silence and Adrienne gathered up the dishes, loaded them on to a tray for Mrs. Ford.

Adrienne went upstairs to her room, turned back the gold quilt, and lay down for an hour. She hadn't been strictly truthful with Mrs. Manning. She had slept rather badly last night. Alone in the small hours she had gone over every word and nuance of those hours with Grant. She shivered at the memory of his touch and its effect on her. He was far too attractive and seemed aware of it. Drat that man, she thought irritably, and fluffed up the pillow. Never again would she give him the satisfaction of ruffling her composure. He even seemed to intrude on her sleeping hours.

Adrienne came back to the present with a start. She really would have to take herself in hand. She was here to work and not to daydream about Grant Manning. She got up quickly from the bed, tidied herself and went in search of Mrs. Manning.

The older woman had already sorted her correspondence and had set aside half a dozen letters for her immediate attention. She greeted Adrienne with a preoccupied smile and gestured her into a chair. "Take some dictation for me, like a darling."

"Certainly, Mrs. Manning." Adrienne drew her chair up closer to the table.

Mrs. Manning dictated briskly but evenly and Adrienne had no trouble in reading back each letter in turn. They had accomplished a fair amount of work when a battery of knocks was launched on the door.

Before Mrs. Manning could answer, Chris Harrington's head appeared around the door, quickly followed by the rest of him. He winked at Adrienne and gathered an unresisting Mrs. Manning into his arms. "The face that launched a thousand fêtes," he murmured, and gave her a resounding kiss.

"Good grief, Chris, I keep waiting for an improvement," she managed, but patted his face with an affectionate hand.

He released her and turned his attention to a smiling Adrienne. "Hello, Adrienne, you beautiful thing, you might as well be in it." He leaned forward and kissed her lightly on the cheek.

"Will you stop, Chris!" his aunt exclaimed. "Take no notice of him, Adrienne, only Grant can control him."

As it happened, Adrienne was not in the least perturbed by Chris's enterprising approach. She smiled back into the audacious blue eyes.

"Adrienne, I'm drowning in those beautiful dark eyes," he groaned.

Mrs. Manning let out a sigh. "We might as well call a halt now, dear, we'll get nowhere with this young man on the premises." It was apparent, however, that she was very pleased to see him. "Are you here for lunch, dear?"

"No, my love," Chris replied breezily, "not today. I thought I'd show Adrienne a bit of the property; in her lunch hour, of course," he added wickedly.

"I don't know about that, dear," his aunt said uncertainly, "After all, Grant would do that, I should think."

"Grant?" he hooted. "He's up to his ears with buyers. I bet he'll swing a nice deal."

"Well, I don't know, Chris. Grant finds time for everything, as you know."

"Oh, don't put me off, dear lady. Adrienne is dying to come with me, can't you see?"

Mrs. Manning exchanged a slightly flustered glance with Adrienne and gave her consent. "All right, then, off you go. Adrienne deserves a break. She's been a great help to me this morning."

Chris gave his aunt another of his effusive kisses, then took Adrienne by the arm. Unlike his cousin, his touch aroused no other sensation than liking for a very likeable young man. They called goodbye to Mrs. Manning and went out to the front of the homestead where a Holden station wagon was parked in the drive. Chris held the door for her and Adrienne slipped into the front seat. He slammed the door shut, walked round to the driver's side and hopped in. "Right-oh! Prepare to enjoy yourself, my girl." Adrienne settled back into the upholstery prepared to do just that.

"Good grief, that's not Venomous Vera's Mercedes, is it?" Chris demanded when they passed a dark green sports model parked at the side of the house. "I didn't notice it when I came in. Is she here?" he queried, his voice rising sharply.

Adrienne, remembering the ruined page of typing she had to re-do, felt inclined to agree with the adjective, but wondered why Chris chose to use it.

"Yes, it's Vera," she replied evenly. "I met Miss Sterling and her brother the other night. I've seen Vera a few times since, but not her brother."

"I'll just bet you have! Our Vera must hate you. She's mad about Grant, as we all know. A looker like you will really throw her." He took his eyes off the drive for a minute and the look he gave Adrienne held both humour and understanding. "I've always looked up to Grant, you know, and he's done a hell of a lot for me. At one time Vera thought he was doing a bit too much and she let me have the benefit of her views on the subject. Phew, what a vixen! I told her if she ever spoke to me like that again, I'd belt her one." He let out an uncomplicated laugh. "We've never been friends since." He slanted a glance full of amusement at Adrienne, and she couldn't help laughing.

"I should think not, Chris. After all, no lady wants to be belted one."

"Seriously though, Adrienne, she could do with it. She's very careful with Grant. Butter wouldn't melt in her mouth most of the time, but fancy getting tangled with her. Grant's thirty-four now, and she hasn't landed him yet. I think she must be getting pretty desperate."

Adrienne thought so too, but didn't mention her

encounters with the lady. It would be better to keep those to herself. They swung out of the main gates past half a dozen cars parked at various intervals and out on to the road. Adrienne sat forward in her seat.

"Handsome devil, isn't he?" Chris remarked at random.

"Who's that?" Adrienne queried, knowing full well there was only one handsome devil.

"Grant, dear girl, and don't tell me you haven't noticed. You would make a stunning couple. It's a good thing I arrived on the scene with my personality." He glanced across at her and Adrienne caught the faintest glimmer of seriousness at the back of his eyes.

She changed the subject. "How far is Careewa, Chris?"

"Just on twenty miles. All this," he continued with an expansive wave of his arm, "is Saranga. Grant has turned it into the finest property of its kind in New South Wales. He's a very respected man out here, and that takes something, let me tell you."

There was considerable pride in his voice when he spoke of his cousin and Adrienne found herself liking him all the more for it. Chris gave credit where credit was due.

It was almost lunchtime and the afternoon promised to be really hot. Sunlight flashed across the windscreen and they both pulled down their visors and laughed. The scent of the stubble paddocks was in the air and the long ribbon of golden brown earth road stretched on and on into the distance. Chris pointed out some drovers shifting a flock of sheep from the rich lucerne pastures into the shade of the Murray pines. He honked the horn in acknowledgement and the lazy-eyed lambs, lifting their heads at the passing car, then butted into one another.

"Have you ever seen the dogs working, Adrienne?"

"Only at the Show, Chris. Everyone turns out to see that."

"Well, you won't have to pay for your entertainment here, though it's a wonder you haven't seen Saranga's

Toby at the Show. I'm almost certain Harry Lawson took him in last year."

"I'll have to be honest with you, Chris, I know little or nothing of country life. I've never been out of the cities. I can see now what I've missed. All this is idyllic."

"Well now, I can hardly wait to show you around. How is the riding going?"

"Oh, I'm progressing, Chris, I think," Adrienne laughed, "but I haven't gone past a canter."

"You soon will," Chris sounded encouraging. "When you're ready for it we'll go boundary riding. It's the best way to see the property. It's beautiful around here, you know. It's in my bones. I could never live in the city, little Miss Brent. I think I would suffocate."

A wallaby hopped across the road and Chris braked suddenly. "Damn him!" he swore under his breath.

"The creek is down there." Chris pointed to where the yellow and grey box thickened. "It's deep enough to swim in, even when it's dry. We'll go down there one day, but we'll need the horses. We might even get a glimpse of the lyre-bird. It has its haunt down there." He turned to the girl at his side. "Don't suppose you've seen one of those either?"

Adrienne smiled and shook her head.

"Well, they're really worth lying in wait for. The tail feathers are gorgeous. Blue and green and gold . . . they sound like a crow one minute, then break out into their famous bell song. I hope we hear it together."

They reached the top of the hill and in the distance was a billowing cloud of dust.

"What's that Chris, another car?"

"No. Saranga stock on the boundary. Grant runs a few head of cattle. The station is self-sufficient, you know. Careewa is on the other side. I run a citrus orchard, oranges and grapefruit. Grant set me up. It's not big yet, but it's a good living. You'll see the groves coming up."

"Oh, Chris, I'd love to, but do you think we should? After all, this is a working day for me."

"Don't worry, girl, Grant doesn't bite. Besides, I want you to meet my mother. You'll love her," he added with absolute certainty in his voice.

Adrienne settled back, but could not dispel the slight feeling of anxiety that crept over her. Grant Manning expected a good day's work, and he certainly paid for it, so she did not think a jaunt around the countryside would please him even if she did have Mrs. Manning's permission. She consoled herself with the thought that he had told her to have the morning off. The speedometer held on seventy and the citrus groves of Careewa came into sight.

"Oh, heavens, Chris, what are those little watch towers? You don't shoot anyone pinching oranges, do you?"

"Those little watch towers, as you call them, dear girl, are wind machines. They prevent damage by frost, convey warmer air from the upper strata, little city slicker. Never let me hear you call them watch towers again."

Chris didn't speak again until they pulled up at the front of Careewa homestead; then he hopped out and came round to Adrienne's side. "Welcome to Careewa, Miss Brent. Not Saranga, I know, nevertheless with a charm of its own."

It was not Saranga. The beautiful lawns and gardens were missing, so too was the old and gracious style of colonial architecture. But in its place was a low bungalow type of building surrounded by flowering shrubs and tall blue gums. Chris was right. It was charming.

"Dad built this. He died in a prisoner-of-war camp – didn't have much chance to live in it. But I like to think he would be happy with what I am doing to it."

Adrienne felt her eyes smart and she covered Chris's hand with her own. "I know he would, Chris. I'm absolutely certain of it."

41

Chris patted her hand, then straightened up. "Right-oh, sweet Adrienne, up you go."

He pulled her up the half dozen steps and as they reached the top the screen door opened and a youthful-looking dark-haired woman came out. "Don't tell me, I know. It could only be Adrienne. You fit Chris's glowing description, my dear."

"Why, thank you, Mrs. Harrington, and so do you," Adrienne smiled.

It seemed to her that Mrs. Harrington resembled Grant – the same blue-black hair and light eyes, although Mrs. Harrington's were as soft and gentle as a dove's. She held back the door and smiled at Adrienne to go in. Adrienne looked around with pleasure. With taste and imagination and considerable housewifely skill, Mrs. Harrington had created a charming and comfortable haven for Chris and herself. All the interior walls seemed to be of pine lining board, but it was waxed lightly to reveal the knots and grain of the timber and looked more effective. The decorating had been keyed to country living and worked out in a cool scheme of blues and greens with a flash of lime and turquoise. Adrienne turned to the older woman, her eyes full of appreciation.

"Knowing Chris as I do, I have lunch ready, so come and have it, both of you," smiled Mrs. Harrington.

She led the way and Chris saw the women seated. A spirit of gaiety pervaded the luncheon table. Mrs. Harrington was in many ways as young and gay as her son and the three of them hit it off remarkably well. Mrs. Harrington seemed much amused when she heard of Adrienne's riding lessons, but added that Adrienne could have no better teacher than Grant. With the Harringtons, at least, Grant Manning could do no wrong. Mother and son kept up a running commentary on the affairs of the district in which Grant figured largely, and Adrienne felt that she had covered a lot of ground in a half hour.

Mrs. Harrington wouldn't hear of Adrienne's helping

with the dishes, but invited her to call over as often as she liked, adding with a laugh that next time she expected to see her on horseback. She waved them both off and once out on the round Chris put his foot down.

"Mum liked you, I knew she would. You should hear her on Vera, but only to me, of course. She loves Grant, but none of us know what he thinks of Vera. He doesn't give much away, our Grant. She's a good-looking girl, mind you, but you sure take the shine out of her."

Adrienne smiled at his choice of words, but didn't pursue the subject. She felt it wasn't altogether advisable to "take the shine" out of Vera Sterling. Vera seemed a ruthless young woman where her own interests were involved.

Chris wanted to know a little about Adrienne's life in Sydney and she presented him with an attractive picture of home which was not altogether accurate. It was difficult to explain Linda, although she seemed to have a counterpart in Vera. The miles flew past and it was just on two when they pulled into Saranga. From the car Adrienne saw Grant in intent conversation with another man and she felt vaguely apprehensive. He had told her to take the morning off, but this was afternoon.

Chris braked, honked the horn at Grant, and opened the door for Adrienne. "I won't get out, Adrienne. I'll have to fly. Be seeing you soon," he called, a little too loudly for Adrienne's comfort, and put the car into motion.

Adrienne turned and walked towards the house and was only two hundred yards away when Grant called out to her, "Miss Brent!" Even at that distance she could see his eyes were like storm clouds and she had the sinking feeling that all was not well. She smoothed her hair unnecessarily and moistened her underlip. The two men were watching her approach and her head came up.

"Yes, Mr. Manning," she replied quietly.

43

"This is Max Blake, one of our American friends . . . my secretary, Max."

Adrienne smiled politely at the other man and she thought that he seemed genuinely disconcerted.

"Your secretary, Grant?" he repeated, then hurried on, "Grant tells me you're a first-class stenographer, Miss Brent, and I need just that. Would you mind doing a few letters for me?"

Adrienne found it hard to believe that Grant had said any such thing, but she replied easily, "Of course, Mr. Blake. When would you like them done?"

"Why, now, Grant, if that's all right with you," Max queried, his eyes on the other man.

"Yes, of course, come along to the office." Grant turned and led the way, going around the side of the house and stood back for them to precede him into the room. "I'll come back. Take your time, Max."

So far Grant hadn't vouchsafed a glance in Adrienne's direction and she knew she wouldn't escape so easily. Max Blake smiled at her and started to pace the room. "Tell me if I'm going too fast," he cautioned kindly, and launched into dictation. As it happened, Adrienne had no trouble in keeping up with him. In fact he dictated rather slowly and disjointedly. He came to a finish and leant against the desk, gazing with open admiration at the young woman behind it.

"How come an extraordinarily pretty girl like you is sitting behind a desk?"

Max was yet another man who didn't equate beauty with brains, Adrienne thought amusedly. She smiled and evaded the question. "I'll type these up for you, Mr. Blake."

"But seriously, though, what do you do out here?" he went on.

Adrienne paused, then answered dryly. "Work mostly, Mr. Blake, but then I've only just arrived."

"Oh," he shrugged, then the obvious thought occurred

44

to him. "Perhaps you could join me for dinner in town this evening?"

Adrienne hesitated on the brink of a pleasant and tactful refusal and found the issue taken out of her hands rather proprietorially.

"I'm afraid that's out of the question, Max," Grant said from the open doorway. "Adrienne doesn't leave the station at night. Just one of the rules while she's under my roof."

"Oh, I see," the American replied equably, without seeing at all. "I guess it's best at that." He winked at Adrienne.

"Come along and have a drink while Adrienne types that up," Grant invited. The two men went out, leaving her free to get on with her work.

About an hour later Grant came in and questioned briefly – "Finished?" Adrienne nodded and he moved forward and took the letters ready for signature, the envelopes neatly attached. "I'll be back," he added, and his tone held an unmistakable note of displeasure.

He was going to be difficult, Adrienne thought, and a tremor ran through her. Ten minutes later he returned and came straight to the point, his tone oddly daunting.

"One, you're not to leave the station without my permission – right," he swept on, without waiting for an answer. "Two, when I tell you to have the morning off, I don't mean part of the afternoon; and three, I won't have you turning Chris's head. I want work from that young man. He's a good boy and very capable, but I can see he's very susceptible to a pair of dark eyes."

He delved in his pocket and brought out a cigarette while Adrienne watched him, temporarily bereft of speech. He lit it, took a deep pull and shifted his gaze back to her through the resultant veil of smoke. "Is that understood?"

Adrienne couldn't believe it, she remained staring up at him for a moment, then rose to her feet in a flurry of

45

words, banging her knee on the desk. Pain made her reckless. "I've never heard anything so damned autocratically unfair in my whole life!" She swallowed, and went on, all caution forgotten. "One," she unconsciously adopted his style, "I'll darned well go where I please in my own time. Two, I spent all morning working for Mrs. Manning and she gave her permission for me to go with Chris. Three, I didn't want to leave the station and the thought of turning Chris's head has just never occurred to me. And four, I've never met such an arrogant, overbearing, highhanded, suspicious minded *beast*!"

Grant came away from the table where he had been leaning, and with one lunge caught hold of her shoulders in a bruising grip. "I'd like to have had the schooling of you, miss, you're nearly uncontrollable." She twisted in his grasp, but he held her fast. "Be still! I'm in no mood to argue with you. You'll do exactly as I say and like it. Is that clear?"

He shook her angrily and Adrienne sank her small teeth into her bottom lip. "Yes, Mr. Manning," she managed through clenched teeth.

"Good, you'll do well to remember it." He made a sound of complete exasperation and let her go. "I don't know what your parents are thinking of, letting you loose. You should be under lock and key for your own protection!"

Adrienne stifled a protest and averted her gaze. She was trembling and the furious tears were close to the surface. For two pins she would throw the whole thing away. One hand clenched and unclenched and Grant's eyes narrowed at the sight of her defiant young face.

He turned abruptly towards the door. "You'd better get on with some work now at any rate," he bit out unfairly, and slammed the door with extreme irritation. Adrienne leant back hard against the table. She felt sick and shaky and suddenly ashamed of her outburst.

How could she have behaved so badly? It could never

have happened with another man. It was just Grant Manning. There was something about him that provoked her beyond all reason. He could be a bit of a beast too. She could still feel his hands on her shoulders. She would bear the marks for weeks. The wonder was he had not dismissed her. There was no following him!

She drew in her breath and turned to the pile of correspondence, working off her tensions pounding the typewriter. At least she got through the work, he couldn't deny that. Adrienne pushed the thought of him resolutely out of her mind and turned her attentions to the typewriter. She had devised a new filing system which wonder of wonders, she thought, had found favour, and there was still a lot to be done on that. It was well after five o'clock before she was finished, and the sun had nearly left the office. Firm footsteps echoed down the hallway and Adrienne stiffened. Was she in for a return bout? she wondered.

"That arrogant, unfair, overbearing beast – was it? – has returned, Miss Brent," he mocked from the doorway.

He looked so infuriatingly handsome, lounging there, that Adrienne had to laugh, if only at herself. "I really must apologise, Mr. Manning. I don't know what came over me."

"Don't you indeed?" he echoed, a glint of devilment in his grey eyes. "I don't know if your apology is accepted then, Miss Brent." He straightened up and came into the room.

Adrienne contrived a nicely off-hand laugh. Her voice was husky. "You did hurt me, you know."

"Not enough, it seems," he answered with just a trace of violence, but he put out a hand to help her up from the chair.

Adrienne willed herself not to go to pieces. She asked quite sweetly, "I'm forgiven, then, Mr. Manning?"

His lean brown hand tightened rather painfully on hers before he relented. "For tonight anyway, my girl," he answered tersely. "Besides, dinner is waiting and I'd hate to sit down in enmity."

Adrienne couldn't look at him. She really needed her running shoes, she thought. This man was dynamite!

He took her elbow and shook her slightly. "Look at me, Adrienne."

She did so, looking rather mysteriously through her heavy dark lashes. He would never guess how her heart was reacting.

Perhaps he did guess, for he dropped his hand and his voice reverted to his usual crisp tones. "You're forgiven, Miss Brent. And now hadn't you better change for dinner? Something mysterious should do nicely."

From her room Adrienne could see Vera's Mercedes still parked at the side of the house. She prepared herself for an uncomfortable encounter.

What did she have that was "mysterious" without being in the least bit . . . dressy? She ran her hand along the line, and then, suddenly piqued by the other girl's attitude, pulled out a cobalt blue paisley chiffon. It was very flattering but very simple in design, depending on Adrienne and the material for its impact. "This should shatter you," she muttered, loath to put a name to whoever it was she intended to shatter.

Mrs. Manning certainly dressed for dinner. No backsliding was tolerated at Saranga. In any case you could hardly sit down in any old thing under a shimmering hand-cut, crystal chandelier.

Adrienne found herself singing soft snatches from Carmen's *Habañera* and broke into laughter. Really, it wasn't as bad as that, was it? With Grant Manning the very air seemed charged with excitement. If she had any sense, she considered, she would go back to Sydney and find a safer job. "Be truthful, Adrienne," she admonished herself. "You're as silly as a rabbit." In any case he was probably used to women collapsing like nine-pins, with his looks and money.

Adrienne finished dressing; carefully checked her lipstick, a soft iridescent pink, then leaned forward into the

48

mirror, subjecting herself to an unusually close scrutiny. She was not vain, but just then she could not help smiling back at her glowing reflection. *"Très bien, mam'selle,"* she whispered, and went out to the dining room.

For some reason which she could not analyse, she felt extremely reluctant to look at Grant, after catching the expression in his eyes as they ran appreciatively over her as she walked into the room. She took her seat beside Mrs. Manning and gave her attention to the iced consommé. Vera was in splendid form. Elegant in white silk jersey, she was witty if somewhat acid in her comments. She looked very lazy and expensive, of which she was both, and mellowed by Grant's attentiveness even managed a few brittle words with Adrienne. Mrs. Manning seemed somewhat subdued and Adrienne turned to her. "You seem a little tired, Mrs. Manning. Is there anything I can do for you?"

"No, thank you, my dear, though it's kind of you to offer. I'm a little fatigued – delayed reaction, I suppose. A good night's sleep should help me." She smiled into Adrienne's concerned dark eyes. "By the way, dear, don't forget you're coming in with me in the morning. It's the Hospital Committee meeting at ten sharp."

"No, of course not, Mrs. Manning. I'm looking forward to it, as a matter of fact. This is all very new and exciting to me out here, you know."

Mrs. Manning studied the girl for a moment. "You know, Adrienne, you look remarkably like what my father used to call a 'hothouse flower' yet you're extremely efficient. The work you did for me was first class. I'm very pleased, my dear."

A soft flush sprang to Adrienne's cheeks. It was very nice to be appreciated.

"What's going on down there?" Grant wanted to know.

"I was complimenting Adrienne on her work, dear. I don't know why it is exactly we should be constantly surprised to find beauty and brains going hand in hand.

49

Just another piece of muddled thinking you men have fostered on us." She laughed in genuine amusement.

"I've no comeback to that, dear Aunt, having three such perfect examples to refute it at my own dinner table."

"Thank you, dear. How gallantly accurate!"

Adrienne lifted her head and at that precise moment encountered such a look of dislike on Vera's face that she felt vaguely repelled. Was she doomed to be forever bracketed with jealous women? Surely I've had enough of that with Linda, she thought.

Grant looked down at the glossy head, seemingly lost in thought. "No opening salvo from you, Miss Brent. I was arming for it."

Adrienne shook off the minute's depression. She answered quite seriously. "I think women take pride in being, to use a word I dislike . . . as decorative as possible. We consider it a feminine responsibility to be maintained. Now that the lordly male has consented to educate his womenfolk, he's been forced into recognising their enormous intellectual potential. You might say that brains and beauty have now become the rule rather than the exception. Man has always been curiously obtuse as far as his better half is concerned."

"Tut, tut!" Grant was doing his best not to laugh. What had started out as a quiet observation ended in an impassioned denouncement. "You don't surprise me, Miss Brent. I might have guessed you would be an ardent little feminist! Just another little woman hellbent on being treated as a little man, all things being equal, of course."

Adrienne sparkled. "You're not the only perceptive one, Mr. Manning. I was quite sure you would agree equality between the sexes is as tiresome as it's mythical."

Grant held her gaze with his own. "Not only mythical, little one, but self-defeating. I would rather love and cherish a woman than have her take over the role. I would much rather provide for her than have her beat me at my own game. A woman's greatest strength is her weakness,

50

you know, Miss Brent, or there's more than the one way to skin a cat."

"Yes, indeed, Mr. Manning. I can quite see that, now that you've been kind enough to point it out to me." Adrienne smiled at Mrs. Manning who was enjoying the exchange. "It's a clear case of let us stoop to conquer."

"Grant's got something there, all the same, Adrienne. I would much rather purr like a cat than roar like a lion." Mrs. Manning arched a delicate eyebrow as though the very idea was the height of absurdity. "Men are the best thing we've got, my dear. There's no getting away from it."

"As if they would ever let us!" Adrienne countered smilingly.

Vera, who had taken a back seat throughout, was noticeably restive. "I wouldn't say beauty was as commonplace as Miss Brent would have us believe," she remarked, looking utterly secure in her own good looks.

"Perhaps not," Mrs. Manning warmed to the subject. "True beauty is rarer than that. Good features are only the foundation. Intelligence, breeding, charm and compassion, warmth and a capacity to love, all these things come in to it." Her gaze rested on Adrienne almost unseeingly. "From the little I've seen of you, my dear, I would say you have the makings of one." At this the colour flooded Adrienne's cheekbones. She was at a loss for words.

Vera's voice was hard and tight. She didn't care for the turn the conversation had taken. "You'll really turn her head, Mrs. Manning. I should think Chris has given her enough compliments already. I couldn't help seeing them in the car."

Mrs. Manning looked across the table at the other girl. Her mouth hardened slightly, but she still smiled. "Trust a young man to appreciate a pretty girl!"

By this time Adrienne was feeling more than a little uncomfortable. She looked briefly at Grant and found his gaze on her. His eyes lingered with appraisal. A little unsteadily Adrienne pushed away her glass and asked Mrs. Manning's permission to look through her record collection, which was extensive and in need of cataloguing. The conversation veered away from the sharply personal and into safer channels. Grant proved to be as knowledgeable as his aunt on the subject of music, and Adrienne was agreeably surprised.

Some of the surprise must have shown on her face, for Grant smiled satirically, his tone frankly mocking. "Why so surprised, Miss Brent? I do find time for life's little refinements."

Adrienne laughed, fairly caught. "I apologise again, Mr. Manning. I'm sure no one could be more suave and polished, but you do give the impression of the great outdoors."

Grant did not contradict the statement but stirred his coffee somewhat vigorously.

Mrs. Manning laughed her agreement, but Vera sprang to the defence of her love. "I don't know how anyone could spend precious time indoors listening to records. I would so much rather be outdoors, and I know Grant would too. When all's said and done I do think it's rather an expensive waste of time."

Mrs. Manning's smile was controlled but expressive. "Well, dear, you're entitled to your opinion, of course, and there would be many to agree with you, but I think you could safely say I'm not one of them."

Vera had sensed she had gone too far with a very important person in Grant's household and she hastened to make amends. "No one could say that *you* spend too much time indoors, Mrs. Manning." She stressed the pronoun placatingly. "I hope you'll forgive my being so candid."

"There's nothing to forgive, Vera." Mrs. Manning answered lightly. "The world will always be divided into two camps, the music-lovers and the non-music-lovers. It's a temperamental thing, I suppose. As you say, you excel in the outdoors." She changed the subject swiftly, turning to the younger girl. "Vera is a champion horse-woman, Adrienne. She takes off all the prizes at the Royal Nationals."

Vera waved a negligent and clearly competent hand. "I hear you're learning to ride, Miss Brent. I could give you a few pointers."

I'll just bet you could, Adrienne thought bluntly, and smiled non-committally at the other girl, loath to take advantage of such a calculated offer.

"What about tomorrow morning?" Vera persisted.

Adrienne wondered how to get out of that one, but Mrs. Manning answered for her, "It will have to be some other time, girls. Adrienne has to come into town with me tomorrow."

"Just as you say," Vera shrugged, and Adrienne felt a sense of reprieve.

She didn't care to be left to Vera's tender mercies, especially as she was coming along so nicely on her own at riding. Though given all the time in the world she would never make a champion horsewoman.

Mrs. Manning rose and took Adrienne off with her to the living room where she kept her record collection. Over her shoulder Adrienne saw Grant draw out Vera's chair and she felt a sharp stab of regret that he did not come too, but was quick to remind herself she must be mad to persist along those lines. If Vera wanted Grant that badly, Vera was welcome to him.

Mrs. Manning and Adrienne settled comfortably into armchairs and relaxed to Moura Lympany's playing of the Rachmaninoff Second Piano Concerto. It was a mutual favourite, even to the interpretation. Half way through the second movement Mrs. Manning came out of her reverie.

"Grant would turn any woman's head. Don't let him turn yours, Adrienne. I know you won't mind my saying so. It's so well meant, my dear. You're very young and I remember what it's like. Vera has waited a long time for Grant and I think he means to marry her, though you

53

never know with Grant. I can't say I like her, but she's a born countrywoman and a good hostess when her emotions aren't involved. She doesn't like you, you're too sensitive not to know that. Steer clear of her, like a good girl." The silver head settled back into the armchair.

Adrienne quelled an impulse to deny Grant's attraction for her, but she knew it would be futile. There was something between them, and Mrs. Manning had already noticed it "I'll remember what you've said, Mrs. Manning, and I'm here to work," she answered quietly.

"Good, dear." The older woman breathed a sigh of thankfulness.

Adrienne closed her eyes, feeling utterly depressed, and let the music roll over her in a triumphant tide.

CHAPTER FOUR

ADRIENNE went down to the office before eight-thirty the following morning to attend to the mail before going into town. She had dressed in a lime silk shirt and a slim navy skirt, and hoped that it would be appropriate. At least, skirts and blouses vaguely filled the working girl role. Quite apart from her good looks, she possessed an undoubted flair for dressing, and her slim-to-the-point-of-slight frame carried clothes extremely well. She wasn't entirely aware of it, although she knew the colour suited her, but the vibrancy of her blouse threw a sheen over her face, deepening the brilliant dark eyes and accenting the red-gold of her hair.

Obedient to the letter, she had drawn it back softly on to the nape of her neck and secured it with a gilt clasp. Perhaps it might be as well to have it trimmed in the town, she considered. The satiny downsurge curving in just free of her shoulders might be all the rage in the city, but it seemed certain Grant Manning didn't care for it. Perhaps one of the new short cuts might suit her.

It was nine-fifteen already. She had better get moving. Adrienne reefed through the mail, sorted it loosely and secured the bundles with Waverley clips. She hoped to be able to attend to it some time that day. With so much work coming in, she couldn't afford to relax on the old. She finished off quickly and presented herself outside Mrs. Manning's study on the dot of nine-thirty.

This morning Mrs. Manning was the first lady to her fingertips. Faultlessly groomed in beige linen with a white panama safari, she made Adrienne conscious of her own bare head.

Evidently Mrs. Manning saw nothing amiss, because she commented briskly, "Oh, you do look nice, Adrienne. You have everything? Pencils, notebooks . . ." Adrienne nodded and indicated her roomy carry-all. "Very well then, dear, we'll go. One of the hands will take us in. Grant said he would pick us up afterwards." She led the way purposefully to the front door and out to the waiting station wagon.

The driver tipped his hat respectfully at Mrs. Manning, but gave Adrienne a knowing wink as she followed the older woman into the car.

There was little conversation on the way into the town. Mrs. Manning seemed more than usually preoccupied. No doubt her mind was on the matters in hand. Adrienne caught the driver's eye in the rear-vision mirror and he gave her another of his cheeky winks. He didn't appear to be very old, nineteen at the most. Adrienne judged him to be harmless, and smiled back. As it happened, this proved to be a mistake, for the station wagon veered sharply to the right-hand side of the road.

"Good heavens, Robbie, do watch where you're going!" Mrs. Manning chided in mild astonishment, then lapsed once more into a thoughtful silence.

Adrienne tried to keep a straight face and looked out the side window, not appearing to notice Robbie's mortified air.

It was just on the half-hour when they turned into the main street of Cooryong. Adrienne was surprised at the size and vigour of the town. The main avenue was lined with pepper trees, and station wagons and stock trucks rumbled past continuously. Cooryong was the centre for a wealthy wool-growing district. Outside the central Post Office was a parklike enclosure bearing a bronze memorial which Adrienne later learnt was erected to the memory of the late Manning brothers who had contributed largely to the prosperity of the town and surrounding countryside.

The street was bathed in brilliant sunshine, and Mrs. Manning waved Robbie off and crossed to an ultra-modern glass-fronted building which bore the name "Manning Memorial Hall" in gold lettering.

The older woman slowed down and turned to Adrienne. "We didn't name it, dear, although Grant put up most of the money for it. All sorts of functions are held here, from weddings to political meetings."

They entered the air-conditioned building and walked up a flight of steps to a smaller committee room. There was a babble of voices ensuing from it which came dramatically to a halt when Mrs. Manning entered.

"Good morning, ladies! All here, I see." She waved a nonchalant greeting here and there and walked up to the dais. Adrienne followed in her wake feeling not unlike a nervous debutante.

"First of all ladies," Mrs. Manning began, "I would like to introduce my off-sider, Miss Adrienne Brent, who is with us at Saranga and is going to take the minutes for us. Then I would like to hear from you."

Adrienne stood up and smiled at the crowded room in general, then sat down quickly. Had she known it, her effect among these hard-working country women was startling. They had long ago accepted Mrs. Manning as the orchid in their midst, but another one—! You could depend on it there would be considerable comment in the homes tonight. The younger women endeavoured to be discreet, but the older ones were openly staring. Adrienne only hoped she passed muster.

Mrs. Manning called the meeting to order and from then on Adrienne was too busy to be left wondering. The project was one dear to the hearts of these women and they were extremely voluble in their comments. Although they deferred to Mrs. Manning as chairwoman and representative of a highly philanthropic family, they all had very definite and sometimes openly conflicting views on what was required and how best to go about the matter of fund-raising. Adrienne's pencil flew along the pages and it was quite one o'clock before the meeting broke up.

Mrs. Manning stood talking to a forceful-looking woman while Adrienne checked over the minutes. There

57

was a burst of laughter from the back of the hall and Adrienne, looking up, caught sight of a sleek dark head towering above the group of chattering womenfolk. Grant was smiling and talking to the women with ease and assurance. He extended to them the utmost courtesy, but the onlooker was aware of his position in the district.

Another peal of laughter went up, and Adrienne frowned in intense irritation. At that precise moment Grant looked up at the dais and caught her unguarded expression. She looked down quickly and gathered her things. Grant broke away from the group with practised charm and came towards the front of the hall.

"Why the ferocious frown?" he enquired, one black eyebrow lifting quizzically.

Adrienne was purposely obtuse. "I didn't know I was frowning, Mr. Manning."

"The lies you tell, Miss Brent!" His eyes narrowed assessingly. "I was watching you."

Adrienne twisted away from him, uncertain beneath his gaze. "Are you leaving for Saranga immediately?" She spoke rapidly.

"Why do you ask?"

"I was thinking of having my hair cut."

"Good grief – why?" His tone was frankly incredulous.

Adrienne hesitated more than a little, surprised by his vehemence. "Well, it appears to annoy you, for one."

His voice grew very dry. "My dear girl, you have beautiful hair, as you very well know."

"I wasn't asking for compliments, Mr. Manning."

"Grant will do. You only do that to annoy me. I'm used to your hair now, let's leave it at that, shall we?" Adrienne drew a long shaky breath and to her astonishment he actually laughed. "We do seem to clash, Adrienne. I wonder why," he added speculatively.

Mrs. Manning hurried up, not wishing to keep Grant waiting. "Hello, Grant dear. Adrienne has been such a help to me. Thank you for lending her to me."

58

Grant turned back to Adrienne and the grey glance slipped over her sardonically. "I think she's happier with you somehow, Helen," he said, holding Adrienne's dark eyes with his own.

Mrs. Manning replied for her. "Adrienne is a girl of spirit, Grant. You do have rather a masterful way, dear. It's only natural for her to resist."

Grant threw up his dark head in mock exasperation. "Good grief, you women! Would either of you care to resist lunch?"

Mrs. Manning smiled fondly back at him and Adrienne found herself relaxing. She always felt so keyed up when Grant was around that she found the time away from him essential to her sense of balance.

He took both women by the arm and escorted them to the adjoining restaurant. It was almost empty, but what people were there obviously knew the Mannings. Grant saw the women seated and walked over to a group sitting along the front window. The hot sun poured over the table and Adrienne wondered why they didn't choose another cooler spot.

Mrs. Manning didn't bother consulting the menu. "I think we'll all have the ham salad, Adrienne, if that's all right with you."

Adrienne nodded. Anything would do, she thought. Grant had taken the edge right off her appetite.

Grant came back to the table. "I know what we're having, ham salad – right?" He looked from one to the other.

Adrienne smiled. "I suppose this has happened before."

"Yes, dear. It's the only thing I'm absolutely happy with." She cast a fastidious look around the small but, to Adrienne, spotlessly clean café.

"What my aunt means, dear girl, in case you're wondering, is she doesn't think they know how to cook."

Lunch was served and it was quite plainly the best the

restaurant could offer. The ham was sliced thickly and the salad was crisp, even if the dressing lacked imagination.

"Take Adrienne along and get some riding gear Helen. I have to go over to the pastoral office. I should be there an hour, so that will give you plenty of time."

Mrs. Manning nodded. "I hadn't forgotten, dear."

Adrienne looked up dismayed. "But I had, Mrs. Manning. I only have about ten dollars on me."

"Good gracious, she's only got ten dollars," Grant remarked maddeningly.

"Stop teasing the girl, Grant. Don't worry about that, Adrienne. It will go on the account."

Adrienne rushed into speech. "Oh, I don't . . ."

"Calm down, little one, the riding gear is on the station," Grant murmured kindly.

Adrienne swallowed on a piece of her roll and subsided. It was useless to argue with him anyway.

He looked sideways at her delicate profile. Adrienne was wearing the sensitive remote air which sometimes came upon her.

Grant laughed. "Yes, it's a shame to tease the baby — Don't worry, Adrienne, we'll exact payment some other way."

Mrs. Manning took command. "Well, if we're finished here, Adrienne and I will go over to Corbans."

Grant paid the bill and they walked out into the dazzling sunshine. It bounced up from the pavement and hit them in the face. Adrienne slipped on her sunglasses. Grant sketched a salute and turned in the direction of the local pastoral agency.

As it happened, Adrienne had little trouble in finding suitable gear. In fact, being so slim she looked well in jodhpurs, though somehow unconvincing. She commented on this to Mrs. Manning, who laughed her agreement.

"Well, now that you mention it, dear, you do look a little fragile. I was never much on a horse myself. I never felt quite safe, being a city girl, I suppose." She laughed a

60

little to herself, her fine blue eyes misted with memories. When they had completed their purchases the two went out into the street.

Grant waved a hand to them from a silver grey Mercedes. Apparently they were in vogue out here, Adrienne thought, with a grin to herself. This one was nearly a match for his eyes, especially when he was angry, as she very well remembered. He got out and opened the door for them, watching the parcels slide across the seat.

Mrs. Manning settled back into the pigskin upholstery and said considerately, "Let's go back the long way, Grant, and show Adrienne the last of the acacias. They've been very late this year because of the frosts."

"I intended to, dear lady. Would you like to sit up the front, Adrienne?"

She raised her eyes to his and they were eager and sparkling. He saw her into the front bucket seat, walked round, got in and switched on the ignition. The beautiful big car purred to life and Grant reversed expertly out of the parking area. The long way proved to be little more than a wide earth road, but the car traversed it smoothly. The wattle lit up the way like lamps.

"The English call it mimosa, don't they?" Adrienne remarked. "It's a lovely name, but I prefer wattle. It spells home. I remember the coster barrows of it in London, but I believe that variety comes from the Mediterranean. It's not nearly so beautiful as ours, nor as prolific."

"You were in London, dear?" Mrs. Manning leaned forward.

"Yes, my father took me on a business trip with him five years ago."

"When you were—?" Grant wanted to know.

"Seventeen, Mr. Manning."

He took his eyes off the road for a moment and Adrienne's pulses leapt at the expression in his eyes. She might as well admit it once and for all and then forget it. She was head over heels in love with him. He had only to look at her for her bones to melt. Thank heaven, she considered, he'd never know it. She wouldn't care to entrust her heart to his lordly keeping.

"What a wonderful experience for a young girl. Did you go over to the Continent, dear?"

"Yes, we had three months there crammed with sight-seeing. Nothing very much really, but Father had to be back in Australia. He remarried not long after." Unconsciously her voice had hardened, and it was not lost on either of the Mannings.

Grant remarked, seemingly at random, "Do you know your Virgil, Adrienne?"

"Well, I do know it has something to do with the Golden Bough."

"Clever girl," he drawled, then went on at a brisker pace. "You will remember that Aeneas found a corner luminous with it in the black wood that stretched before the gates of Hell. He broke off a branch as a talisman and crossed the Styx."

"Good heavens, that's interesting, Grant. I never knew that," Mrs. Manning replied artlessly, and both Grant and Adrienne laughed.

"There's nothing like a bit of culture, dear aunt. It's all for Adrienne's benefit, of course. She sometimes looks at me as though I'm a barbarian and she's the patrician princess."

They all laughed and Grant pulled the car off the wide track and got out. He crossed over to a giant cootamundra, broke off a bough and came back to the car. "There you are, Adrienne . . . a talisman." His voice was light, but his eyes were strangely watchful.

She looked down at the gauzy smother of leaf, the miniature constellations frail as a dandelion and the quick emotional tears loomed close to the surface. She looked up at him, found him so close that she could see the tiny golden flecks in his irises and her breath caught. "How lovely!"

Mrs. Manning watched the little scene with a growing sense of anxiety. Didn't Grant realise how attractive he was, especially to a girl of Adrienne's temperament? She could only get hurt, and Mrs. Manning found herself very much against such an eventuality. Why, only this morning dear Vera had hinted at an announcement in the not too distant future. Devil take the girl! Try as she would, she couldn't stand her.

"We'd better make tracks, Grant," she remarked lightly, and he came back to the driver's side and put the car in motion. No one spoke for the remainder of the journey and when they arrived back at the homestead, Adrienne carried the golden cloudburst up to her room.

The following day Grant flew to Sydney for the wool sales. Adrienne had seen the giant bales standing as high as a man loaded on to semi-trailers during the week. Unlike wheat, wool was a light and valuable enough freight to make extensive use of road transport. Each bale was stamped with the name MANNING–SARANGA and the station number, although the same process would be repeated at the receiving points.

Grant was expected to be away three or four days. Adrienne supposed he would be interested in the best price he could get for his wool as well as the cheque to cover his future commitments. She had no idea what a wool sale would be like. She did know that they accounted for more than ninety per cent of the Australian clip, the largest in the world. Adrienne knew that Grant was a member of the National Wool Board, and she had typed out articles for him on promotion, testing and marketing, and had filed considerable correspondence from textile manufacturers. She determined to make a study of the whole thing while he was away.

Adrienne found a note from Grant propped up on the desk when she went through to the office, and glanced through it quickly. It certainly bore out the theory that one's writing was indicative of the personality. Grant's script was firm and well-formed, dashing and completely confident – the writing of a man of action with a surprising imaginative bent. She found herself smiling at it and immediately made a small grimace. Lord, she was becoming simple-minded about the man. Smiling at his writing! What next!

She turned back to the desk. Well, he had left her plenty to do, and no doubt would expect it to be done when he returned, whenever that would be. Adrienne sat down at the typewriter.

"I wonder how he'll fill in the evenings." She lapsed into daydreams. Grant would make a superb escort. The old cliché suggested itself irresistibly . . . tall, dark and handsome. She tossed back her hair impatiently and put paper in the machine.

Mrs. Manning came in at lunchtime and invited her to share her chicken sandwiches. Adrienne guessed correctly that the older woman was sometimes lonely for the companionship of her own type of woman. Despite the big gap in their ages, they found themselves able to converse easily and freely.

Mrs. Manning managed to slip into the conversation that Vera had flown back with Grant . . . for the trip and the bright lights. She had definitely developed a protective attitude towards Adrienne. As far as Mrs. Manning was concerned, no girl in her right mind would poach on Vera's preserves. How could Grant be so blind, she thought, though Vera was honey itself where Grant was concerned. She could only put in a warning word here and there.

Later on in the day there was a call from Careewa. Adrienne answered the phone and listened to Chris's pleasant nonsense, then handed the receiver over to Mrs. Manning.

Fifteen minutes later Mrs. Manning came into the living room where Adrienne was kneeling in front of the stereogram, sorting records. "I've invited Marion and

Chris for the week-end." She sank into an armchair. "I worry about Marion, you know. She's made Chris her whole life and she's too young and attractive to do that. It's no life for a woman on her own. And she's so talented too. One of these days Chris will marry, and there you are."

"Chris told me about his father. What a tragedy!" Adrienne said quietly.

"Yes, dear, a tragedy, as you say. There have been a few of them in this family." Even now, years later, there was a hint of strain in her voice. Adrienne was suddenly conscious of the truth of this statement and she looked down at the records. What was there to say? A loss was a loss and absolutely final. She should know.

"Well, we can't dwell on the past, dear. As I say, they'll be here for the week-end." She rested her silver head on the wing of the chair. "Marion has a sister in Sydney. She should go back there. I think she will when Chris marries. I certainly will whenever Grant takes a wife."

Adrienne received this piece of information in silence. The thought of Grant's taking a wife was too awful to dwell on.

"There's quite a family resemblance between Grant and Mrs. Harrington, isn't there?" She changed the subject.

"Yes, there's the colouring, of course. It's so unusual . . . that dark hair and light eyes. Paul and Stephen were the same. Grant is very fond of Marion and she of him. He'll always look after her, and Chris too. Though thank heaven, Chris is a man. He's got good blood in him, that boy."

Adrienne laughed. She couldn't help it. Good blood all right, and running pretty fast! Mrs. Manning, listening to the infectious lilt, laughed too. Adrienne went back to sorting the records and the two of them lapsed into a relaxed silence interspersed with light easy conversation. It was a pleasant evening and mutually they agreed on a ten o'clock bedtime . . .

Next morning Adrienne rose early, spent an hour with

Gemma and started on the lengthy and involved task of cataloguing Mrs. Manning's extensive record collection. She devoted nearly two hours to it and then turned to the never-ending filing. It was quite noon before she had things under control. Mrs. Manning had asked her to cut some flowers for the house in the late afternoon and she found herself looking forward to it with pleasure.

About five-thirty she wandered out into the gardens which lay on either side of the drive, collected a large flat-bottomed basket and the secateurs from old Mee Lee, the Chinese gardener, who had been on the station for years. At the back of the homestead in a sheltered court-yard was the rose garden, and this she left until last. In no time at all the basket was filled with a riot of colour and fernery and she went through the white lattice archway to the roses. They were nodding their lovely heads to the evening breeze.

Adrienne's spirits soared. This was a little like Beauty and the Beast. He seemed a little hostile at the idea of actually cutting his prize blooms. Adrienne cut with abandon. To the pinks and golds and crimsons she added a dozen perfect Virgos. She had a special love for white flowers. It was a heady sensation to be among so many. By the time she had finished it was almost dusk and the pink flame had left the sky.

Adrienne dawdled a little on her way back to the house, until she saw Mrs. Manning leaning against the wrought iron railing obviously waiting for her.

"How lovely! I'll leave you to arrange them, dear. I just know you're artistic."

Adrienne smiled. "I'll do my artistic best. May I have the Virgos for my room, Mrs. Manning?"

"Of course, dear, of course. Come in now. Marion and Chris will be here in time for dinner."

Adrienne went through to the kitchen and asked Mrs. Ford's permission to use a free bench. She selected appropriate recepticles, including a huge bronze kettle

66

that had been brought back from Morocco, and went to work. Mrs. Ford actually found herself devoting more time to watching the various arrangements take shape than to the preparation of the dinner.

"You've a way with flowers and no mistake," she commented.

"I'm glad you think so, Mrs. Ford." Adrienne sketched a hand over the top of the bases.

"They look like they grew there. Mine always look like they're longing to be back in the garden."

Adrienne smiled. She was rather pleased with the results herself, although she had everything at hand to make for success. "I'll take them through, then I'd better get dressed." At the doorway she turned. "Not everyone can cook like you, Mrs. Ford. I'll surely put on weight here!"

Mrs. Ford studied the slight young figure consideringly. "Well, there's little enough of you, but I'm glad you appreciate good food."

"Oh, I do," Adrienne laughed, and disappeared with her fragrant load.

She had just started dressing when she heard Chris's signature tune played out on the horn of the Holden. She could see his mother trying to stop him – unsuccessfully, too, it would seem. She smiled to herself and reached behind her back to zip up her dress. It was pale blue crêpe appliquéd with navy scrollwork at the neck and hem.

Adrienne could hear the two women laughing as she went out to the living room – probably, she thought, at one of Chris's uninhibited observations.

"Adrienne, you gorgeous creature! We've been waiting for you." He drew her into the room with smiling enthusiasm. "Isn't she a beautiful girl!" He turned to the two older women.

"You've my permission to squash him on all occasions, Adrienne," Marion laughed. "I've heard nothing else but Adrienne all week."

Chris put a sherry into her hand. It was sweet, but she

drank it. Dinner was faultless and they chatted happily through the asparagus, spring chicken and pineapple fritters with apricot sauce.

"That Mrs. Ford is a treasure," Chris rhapsodised through a second helping of the dessert snowed under with whipped cream.

"The poor lad doesn't eat at home," his mother explained kindly. Indeed Chris was giving every appearance of not doing so.

Later on when Mrs. Ford came in with the coffee Chris complimented her extravagantly, but she merely smiled over his head at his mother. She was a woman of few words. The hands of the clock flew round and it was well after midnight before they had all settled for the night. Adrienne lay awake for a while watching the shifting pattern of moonlight across the room. Chris had looked unusually serious when he had promised her a picnic the following day, which was now today, Adrienne thought drowsily. The light from the hall had shone on his fair head but his eyes had been in the shadow. Perhaps it had been a trick of the light. Adrienne plumped up her pillow and turned her face into it. "I hope he doesn't become serious," she thought on the borderline of sleep. She would have to see that didn't happen.

Morning dawned over Saranga bright and clear. After breakfast, Chris went through to the kitchen to marshall Mrs. Ford's resources for the promised picnic.

It was the right day for it, although it was still enough to suggest there could be a storm by evening. He hoped not. In any case he would have Adrienne home long before then. By about ten-thirty they were ready. One of the roustabouts, who turned out to be Robbie, let down the sliprails for them and put them up after they had passed through. Adrienne smiled at him and Chris leaned out of the saddle to have a few words with him. Evidently they knew one another quite well.

Gemma followed Chris's lead of her own accord. Adrienne could see that all she had to do was keep her seat and enjoy herself. The morning smelt exhilerating and they cantered through the apple orchard watching the hawks circling in the limitless blue sky. Now and again they smiled at one another or Chris turned to point out something of interest, but in the main they were silent, enjoying the clarity of the morning.

The crows were out in force this morning, setting up their raucous din. They rode on for about an hour, opening and shutting innumerable gates, and presently came to the foot of a steep little hill almost completely covered in boulders.

Adrienne turned to Chris. "How do we get around this?"

"We don't, my sweet. We ride up to the top and down the other side."

"You're joking, Chris. It's almost perpendicular!"

"Come on!" he shouted, and before she knew what had happened Gemma had started the ascent, picking her way carefully between the boulders until they reached the top.

Adrienne couldn't believe she was there, neither did she fancy the descent, but the view was magnificent. Saranga homestead, the heart of the sheep station, nestled in the centre of the valley guarded by the great wooded mountains. Spread out across the countryside were the merinos feeding on the lush lucerne pastures. Away from them, in a splendid little kingdom of their own, were the brood mares and their foals running against the trees. A few clouds had come up and skuddered off to the larkspur mountains. It was an enchanting scene to delight the eye; a golden sun-drenched pastoral. A colony of cicadas shot up into the sky, singing away their short lives.

A feeling of utter strangeness came over Adrienne. She turned to Chris. "The vision splendid! Thank you for bringing me."

Chris baulked at anything flowery. "Yes, it's nice all right." He smiled at her, settled his hat back on his head and started to make the descent. On the other side, under the tall eucalypts, came a constant shower of blossoms. Chris followed a pad through the tall trees until they came to the lip of the gully.

"We'll dismount here, Adrienne." He swung off his horse, helped Adrienne down and took both bridles. "It's a bit tricky from here on. We'll have to go on foot. I'll just tether these two."

Adrienne watched him and dug her heels into the thick springy grass. She looked round her with pleasure. The air was like incense with the smell of the glade. It reached out to her with its cool lushness, and was so pleasant after the heat of the sun. She could hear the murmur of the water in the grotto that tunnelled under the overhanging foliage. Ferns and creepers sprung in profusion and underfoot the earth was damp where the sun had not penetrated the dense greenery. Intermittent sunlight quivered on the dew damp leaves, setting them a-sparkle.

Chris came back to her and took her by the arm. "Just follow me and we'll go down there." He indicated a tricky path and she followed close behind him.

"Where are we going, Chris?"

He put up a warning hand. "Ssh! We'll frighten off our friend."

Adrienne quietened and Chris found a woody shelf screened by thick ferns. He made a place for them both. "We might be here for some time, so make yourself comfortable."

Chris stretched himself out and after a while Adrienne did the same. Here and there the sun dappled the ground, but mostly the glade was dim and moist.

Adrienne closed her eyes. Now and again a berry plopped to the ground. She was completely at peace. Chris raised himself on his elbow and looked down at the enchanting face. How lovely she was, he thought, and how unaware of him. Oh well, I'll have to work at it, he thought, and leaned back and waited.

About twenty-five minutes later a shrill cackle pierced the air.

"Adrienne!" Stealthily Chris parted the ferns and Adrienne edged forward leaning across his arm. There, with the lush glade for a backdrop, was the lyrebird. He was cawing away; then, seemingly touched by a Svengali, chimed into his pure clear song. As though he knew he had an audience, he stalked into the middle of the clearing and elevated his gloriously iridescent tail feathers. Even in that dim place they glowed with a life of their own, held aloft in a conglomeration of shimmering beauty. It was a wonderful show of blue, green and gold with the softest of browns. Silently they watched him. He chimed again.

"Oh, Chris!" Adrienne couldn't help herself. Immediately the bird threw off its regal pose and clucked off into the bush, reduced to a fowl.

"Weren't we lucky?" Chris scrambled up and gave her his hand. He released her and Adrienne brushed herself down. She was covered with twigs and bits of fern. They tracked back to the horses and Chris led the way out of the glade.

"We'll have lunch at the next rise." Adrienne nodded happily. She rode on for a while, bare-headed, then adjusted the strap of her cream felt. The sun's rays were too powerful to be without a hat for long. In the natural clearings kangaroos grazed or popped leisurely into the scrub. Adrienne was fascinated. She had never seen a kangaroo outside the zoo.

"Aren't the sheep afraid of them, Chris?" she asked.

"Heavens, no, they take one another for granted." He pointed to a mother kangaroo with a joey in its pouch. "Look lovely, don't they, and so harmless. Yet you wouldn't credit the amount of damage they can do. They can amount to a menace. All the same I hate shooting them. But don't let's talk about that."

He got a grip on the reins and put his mount to the gallop. At the top of the rise he pulled off his hat and started waving it in the air. An unearthly yodelling rent the silence of the bush. Adrienne laughed and rode up to him, the long grass swishing under Gemma's hoofs. She looked back on a trail of flattened buttercups. There was no need to tell Chris she was stiff. That would brand her a real city slicker! She slid out of the saddle feeling very professional indeed.

"Bet you're stiff," Chris grinned at her.

"Don't tell me it shows! I was just congratulating myself."

"You were drooping a little bit," he laughed, "but don't worry, it soon wears off. You're doing very well." He collapsed on the ground. "Gosh, I'm hungry!"

"Your mother must be flat out feeding you, Chris."

"I'm a big boy. Adrienne," he drawled, and pushed his hat down over his eyes.

"Well, what have we got here?" Adrienne laid out Mrs. Ford's feast. She was hungry herself. There was one large plastic tablecloth – they couldn't eat that. One thermos! Ah, this was more like it. Chicken, boiled eggs, tomatoes, a little crisp lettuce heart, dressing, what was this – potato salad, and some rolls and fruit. A feast indeed.

"What's in the thermos, Adrienne? I hope it's not coffee. It's too hot."

Adrienne unscrewed the lid. "We're in luck, it's snickeny cider."

"Good grief, not cider?"

Adrienne laughed out loud. "Sorry, Chris, I think it's lemonade."

Chris rolled over and found the paper cups. "Good, I'll have a drink of that." Adrienne set out the food on the disposable plates and passed Chris his giant-sized portion. "Oh, this is the life, Adrienne! I wonder what the poor people are doing."

Adrienne looked over at him. He was very likeable. He met her gaze head on. "Oh, Adrienne, a glass of lemonade, a horse and thou beside me in the wilderness!"

Adrienne laughed and shifted over so that her back was against the trunk of the gum tree. "Where did you go to school, Chris?"

Chris crossed over to the horses and came back with a small rug. "Here, put that behind you." He folded the rug and slipped it behind Adrienne's back. "Well, I learnt a lot the two days I was there." He picked up the conversation.

Adrienne laughed. "Seriously, Chris, where did you go to school?"

He mentioned a well-known public school and they drifted into talk of the not-too-distant school days. After lunch, drowsy with the heat and the food, they lay down under the shade of the trees and had a nap.

About twenty minutes later Adrienne opened her eyes, completely refreshed, and found that Chris was unhitching the horses.

"How did you know I would wake up just then?"

"I was watching you."

"You're not supposed to do that."

"What?"

"Watch someone when they're sleeping."

"Why ever not? You want to come over and see some of my hands. I get in a lot of practice that way."

Chris held the stirrup and Adrienne found herself vaulting into the saddle. She was getting cheeky.

"There's no need to show off."

"Oh, Chris, you seem to echo what I'm thinking." Her dark eyes sparkled up at him from under the wide brim of her hat.

"Oh, lord!" he sighed out loud.

"What's up, Chris?"

"Nothing to worry you, miss. Let's get cracking." They mounted and set off.

"Do you think you could settle out here, Adrienne?" he asked presently.

"I've never thought about it, Chris."

73

"I suppose for a city girl it would be much too quiet."

"Oh, I wouldn't say that, Chris. It's really beautiful out here and there must be tons to do on the station."

"Oh, yes, tons of work, but I mean in the way of entertainment."

"I'm not wildly social," she told him. "I never have been, although I do like to dress up and go out occasionally."

He turned and considered her. "No, you don't seem the social butterfly, but you're certainly beautiful enough to be one."

Adrienne twinkled at him. "No more compliments, please, Chris, or I'll fall out of the saddle!"

He slanted her a bright glance and lapsed into a companionable silence. A good way off a cloud of dust seemed to be moving towards them.

"Stock, Chris."

"Not this time, city girl," he laughed. "That's a road over there. It's a car – probably the Donaldsons'."

They rode over and reined in beside the road. The driver of the car slowed down and came to a stop beside them. A pretty young face put its head out the window, the ready smile fading a little when it came to rest on Adrienne.

"How goes it, Chris?"

"Well, speak of the Saints! Where have you been, Freckles?" he grinned. "This is Adrienne, Grant's secretary – Tammy Donaldson, Adrienne, known to her friends as Freckles."

"No one has called me Freckles for years now but you, Chris," Tammy burst out indignantly. She acknowledged the introduction pleasantly, but Adrienne was aware of her close scrutiny. "Mum was saying you took the minutes for Mrs. Manning the other day. She didn't exaggerate about your looks either."

"Thank you, Tammy," Adrienne replied.

The girl turned back to Chris. "I've been in the big city

with Rene and the baby. When are you coming over to see us?"

"Soon, Tam. How is Rene? What is it, a boy or a girl? Bound to be one or the other."

"Oh, Chris!" Tammy let in the clutch, exasperated. "Come over and bring Miss Brent if she'd like to come."

She waved a hand and moved off slowly so as not to raise a dust. On the side of the road Adrienne and Chris watched the car receding.

"You've got a fan there, Chris." It was quite apparent he only saw Tammy as the Freckles of his childhood. It wouldn't hurt to point it out, Adrienne thought.

"You're joking," he said, but his eyes were suddenly speculative. The idea was evidently not in the least tasteful. Adrienne smiled to herself and they continued on through the afternoon. Chris pointed out all the Saranga landmarks and even encouraged her to leave Gemma to go at a gallop. But this time Adrienne felt reasonably in harmony with the horse's movements and felt confident enough to try it.

"Let's stop for a cool drink," Chris called, and reined in. He stooped and pulled a swatch of grass and absent-mindedly began to wisp his horse.

Adrienne passed him a paper cup. "Here we are. Chris." He drank the lemonade down thirstily and Adrienne said a little anxiously, "I think we'd better be moving, Chris, they look like storm clouds to me on the horizon."

"They are. I've been looking at you instead of them." He handed her up and swung into the saddle.

They cleared the rise and Adrienne felt a twinge of alarm. She hadn't noticed the length of the ride out because she had been enjoying herself so much, but it looked a long way in and those clouds were banking ominously. They rode on in silence and within half an hour came the first drum roll of thunder. Gemma threw up her head and fidgeted with the bit.

"Oh, lord, Adrienne, I am sorry. We're going to be caught in it." He sounded so contrite that Adrienne laughed.

"It's not the first time I've been caught in a thunderstorm, Chris. What about the horses?"

"They'll be all right. It's you I'm worried about."

The violent summer lightning flashed across the sky and then the rain came down. Big single heavy drops at first, then all at once flung out of the heavens wholesale. By this time Adrienne was frightened, though she tried hard not to be. The lightning was bad and Gemma seemed to be bunching her muscles on the point of acting up. Adrienne was sure she wouldn't be able to hold her. "Is there anywhere we can shelter her, Chris?" she shouted.

"No, worse luck. We can't go near the trees, not with this lightning."

Helplessly they gazed at one another through the heavy veil of rain, the lightning playing about over their heads.

"I'd laugh, Chris, if I wasn't so darned wet."

"We'll make for the road." He swung over, then grasped Gemma's bridle, turning her head around. By the time they reached the road the worst of the storm seemed to be over; there were only intermittent flashes and the rain was easing off. They lifted their heads sharply at the sound of an engine.

"Lord, we're for it! That's the land rover. Grant must be home."

Grant it was. He swung out of the vehicle, lean and dark and frowning. "Catch these, Chris. I thought you had more sense!" He turned to Adrienne and swung her urgently out of the saddle. She swayed and he kept a steadying arm around her.

Chris had struggled into the oils and pulled the hood down over his head. "I'll get the horses back, Grant," he called placatingly, and veered off across the paddocks.

Grant leaned into the land rover, bundled the drenched girl into a lightweight rug from the back seat, and almost flung her across the seat. He got in after her and pulled down the side flap.

Inside the land rover it was warm and intimate, and Adrienne wished it was possible to extend the moment endlessly. Grant's eyes travelled over her. "Haven't you any sense at all?"

"I don't know what you mean," Adrienne defended herself. "It was great fun."

He glanced deliberately at the soft sheen of her mouth which had long since lost its lipstick, and she coloured and answered crossly, "Not that sort of fun."

"I'm glad to hear it," he commented dryly. His hand shot over to the back seat and came back with a towel. It was gorgeous! Pale blue roses rioted over a sapphire background, thickly piled and expensive.

Adrienne draped it over her head and burst out laughing. "Is this yours, Grant?"

He turned and looked at her. Her skin was pearly with the rain, the brilliant blue of the towel deepening her sparkling eyes to black. At the quality of his silence her laughter stilled and she moistened her soft pink mouth with the tip of her tongue. Grant moved. He brought up one hand and tapped her sharply on the side of the cheek.

"Ooh! What's that for?" Adrienne gasped, and put a hand to her smarting face.

"For being out in the rain," he admonished, and sent the car forward.

Adrienne pulled the towel off her head and began to dry it. It took some time, then she turned towards him. "You're back early. We didn't expect you."

Grant spoke briefly. "Be still, child." Adrienne's breath caught. He transferred his gaze momentarily from the road. "Be quiet, there's a good girl, or you'll have me running off the road."

Adrienne subsided. Well, really! Running off the road! How could she? It had stopped raining and in any case he was an excellent driver. She moved conspicuously over to the far corner of the land rover and turned her head. Did she imagine it, or had Grant stifled a laugh. Not far from the homestead a giant tree had come down and lay neatly cleaved down the centre. They pulled into Saranga Homestead and Grant sent her up before him.

"Have a hot bath and for heaven's sake dry your hair properly. That was a token performance in the car."

Adrienne ran up the stairs where Mrs. Manning and Marion were both waiting. "We were so worried," they greeted her.

"I'm sorry," Adrienne apologised. "But it was great fun – even the storm. Chris should be here soon, Mrs. Harrington. He's bringing the horses."

"Get moving, Adrienne." Grant took the stairs two at a time. She obediently took to her heels. As she passed the mirror in her room she couldn't help noticing how intensely alive she looked. All for Grant, of course. She felt happy and excited and completely unsettled. This was madness. Didn't he call her "child" in that maddeningly patronising way? She turned on the hot shower and revelled in it.

Afterwards, because it was still muggy, she took out a cream cotton voile sprigged with white rosebuds. It was one of the few dresses in her wardrobe that was belted. Most of the others were smocks. She tightened the belt around her narrow waist and patted down a fold of the full skirt. Now that she looked at herself it was a wonder she stuck so slavishly to the fashions. She was inclined to agree with her father that there was nothing more feminine than a small waist and a billowing skirt. She took a pair of strappy sandals out of the bottom of the wardrobe and stepped into them, then went out through the house. Marion and Grant were deep in conversation and she hesitated, not wishing to intrude on them.

"Oh, there you are, Adrienne. You look like a flower come in out of the rain," Marion remarked somewhat poetically.

78

Grant let a few seconds elapse before he added very dryly, "And your hair all caught up too so we won't know if it's dry or not."

Adrienne walked into the centre of the room. "I never catch cold, you know," she informed them seriously, then sneezed.

Marion pealed into laughter. "Heaven help you if you do! Grant is a tyrant and he'll expect you to type on regardless." She threw him an indulgent look, then leant over and patted the lean brown hand.

Adrienne watched him return the affectionate gesture, then he moved off the arm of the sofa to the cabinet. "What will you have, Adrienne?"

Adrienne glanced down at the two crystal tumblers on the table. "Scotch on the rocks, please, with just a little water."

One black eyebrow flew up. "You're joking."

"No, I'm quite serious. I'm over twenty-one, you know."

"Are you really, Adrienne?" Marion sidetracked. "You don't look it."

"She doesn't act it either," Grant said crisply, and mixed the weakest of whiskies. He came back to her, waiting expectantly in the middle of the room. "One of these days, I'll let you have a few drinks, but not now," he added repressively. "Sit down, child." Yes, that was exactly how he saw her – as a "child!"

Marion patted the cushion of the long divan and Adrienne walked over to her, her skirt swinging in a graceful arc. "What a pretty dress, Adrienne," Marion fingered a fold of the material. "I'm not altogether keen on these smocks. It's hard to tell what sort of figure a girl has."

"Oh, I wouldn't say that." Grant observed laconically, and the smile sounded in his voice. Adrienne looked across at him and saw his eyes on her. She looked away quickly.

"Is Chris back, Mrs. Harrington?"

"Yes, dear, and Marion will do. It makes me feel old to have a young thing like you call me Mrs. Harrington."

"Why, thank you, Marion." Adrienne felt herself warming to the other woman's charm. These Mannings had it in abundance.

Mrs. Manning came into the room beautifully groomed as usual, her ice blue linen showing not the sign of a crease. Adrienne allowed herself a slight smile at the thought of ever calling Mrs. Manning "Helen". It was unthinkable. She was too much the *grande dame*.

"None the worse for your soaking, Adrienne?" She sank into the armchair. "You can hear Chris singing, if we're going to be charitable, all over the place. The rain must agree with you young people. Thank you, dear." She took her drink off Grant and sipped it appreciatively. "What is this, Grant, brandy, lime and soda?"

"No, darling, rock and rye. You get caught every time. I can't for the life of me think why."

"Well, they all taste the same, don't they?" Mrs. Manning passed it off somewhat inaccurately. "I'm simply dying for the piano to arrive. Adrienne plays. It will be lovely to have some music in the house."

Adrienne smiled at her and looked up from her empty glass. "May I have another one please, Mr. Manning? For medicinal purposes, of course." Her eyes held a spice of mischief.

He took the glass from her and gave her finger a sharp pinch as he did so.

"Oh, you have got a sadistic streak!" Adrienne withdrew her hand quickly.

He refilled her glass then came back to her. "That's your last, or heaven knows what you'll be saying about me."

"When do you expect it to arrive?" Marion wanted to know.

"What, dear?" Mrs. Manning came back from wherever she was.

"The piano," Marion laughed.

"Oh, I don't know, dear. I just told them to send it." She waved a fine-boned hand. "It could take time, I suppose."

Marion was just about to ask Adrienne where she had had her training when Chris made his exuberant entrance. "Here I am, suave, immaculate and somewhat battered!" He threw out a hand with a badly-skinned knuckle.

Adrienne got up immediately and went over to him, her face concerned. "Oh, Chris, show me. How did you do that?" She bent over his hand.

"Hang on, dear girl, and I'll go out and batter the other one."

"He'll survive, Adrienne, no need to sympathise with him." Grant came over and took his cousin by the shoulder. "I've got some film from Primary Industries I want to show you later on."

"Oh no, Grant, have a heart! Adrienne and I are going to do all the latest dances. She's learnt to waltz."

Grant laughed at him and said no more for the time being.

Mrs. Ford had surpassed herself, no doubt in honour of the master of Saranga's return. Adrienne bent her head over her plate and suppressed a smile. Life was going to be one long banquet out here. All the passion of a lifetime was channelled into Mrs. Ford's cooking. She couldn't help it, but she laughed out loud. There was a lull in the conversation and everyone looked at her.

"What's up with you, dark eyes?" Chris queried.

"I was thinking how many banquets I've had out here."

Mrs. Manning looked over at her, surprised. She had long since become accustomed to the excellence of Mrs. Ford's cooking. In fact, she took her very much for granted. "I suppose we do have a marvel in the kitchen. Thank goodness!" she added piously. "I can't boil an egg, although they tell me it's very difficult."

Chris screamed, "Who tells you?"

"Oh, it's in all the magazines. I'm forever reading it's the true test of a cook or something."

"Oh, surely not, Helen." Marion was clearly amused.

"I think you mean boiling potatoes, Mrs. Manning." Adrienne was trying to be helpful.

"Oh, for heaven's sake, let's get off such a dreary subject," Grant said adamantly.

Adrienne was still laughing and sounded so amused that Chris started to laugh too.

"What's going on at my dinner table?" Grant looked up. "I think you've had too much to drink, Adrienne." She glanced over at him quickly, but his mouth was amused. Maybe she had, she certainly felt wonderfully happy.

After dinner Chris went over to the radiogram and looked through the pile of records. "Stone the crows! We'll go well with these. Khachaturian, Rachmaninoff, Albeniz, Liszt, Chopin." He rifled through a dozen more. "Good grief, not Bach too!" He looked over at his aunt. "Forgive me, dear lady, for my despondency, but is this all you've got to dance to?"

"Oh, Chris!" Mrs. Manning just laughed. Then she brightened. "There's a Julian Bream."

"Don't put me off with one of your new liqueurs!"

"Julian Bream, Chris, the guitarist." Adrienne was on the verge of the giggles.

"Too romantic," Grant threw in. "You're both getting out of hand as it is."

"Romantic, eh? Come on, Helen, get it out." Mrs. Manning crossed to the radiogram, but Adrienne got there before her.

"I'll find it for you, Mrs. Manning." She knelt on the floor beside Chris, her skirt spread out around her. "Here it is. You've mixed these up, Chris." She righted a few records.

Chris took the Julian Bream and put it on the turntable. The record fell down and the haunting *Granada* from the

Suite Espagnole slipped into the room. "My goodness, someone's off their pins! What could you do to that?" Chris was disgusted.

Adrienne looked into Grant's enigmatic light eyes and hoped he would never guess the thought that flashed into her head. Chris went to turn it off.

"Oh, leave it, Chris, it's heavenly." Mrs. Manning wasn't going to be put off.

"He's marvellous on the lute too," Adrienne remarked.

"He'd need to do something besides play the guitar." Chris was definitely not impressed.

"Oh, Chris!" Adrienne collapsed back into the sofa.

He turned on his cousin. "I like your idea of 'romantic', Grant. You'll do no good out here." For once Grant had no reply, but turned with a laugh and went out of the room.

"Oh, Chris, you should see your face. It's comical!" Adrienne gave a soft mirthful giggle.

"My boy's not a music-lover, Adrienne. He takes after his father in that way." Marion was enraptured with the round caressing tone of the master guitarist.

"Come on, my lad, duty calls." Grant came back into the room with a spool of film. "Leave the ladies to their simple pleasures."

"Well, things being what they are, Adrienne's missed the thrill of a lifetime "

"There'll be other times, Chris," Adrienne promised consolingly.

"Will there, miss?" Grant cocked a quizzical eyebrow.

"You bet there will!" Chris put in feelingly.

"Take him away, Gray. I'm trying to listen." Marion lifted her head from the back of the armchair. "He's a real Dennis the menace."

"Come on, Dennis." Grant propelled his mildly protesting cousin out of the living room. For the better part of the evening, the three women had the room to themselves. Adrienne put on records as the other women requested them and told them about her Conservatorium days.

About half-past nine, Mrs. Manning asked Adrienne to see if Grant and Chris wanted supper.

"Chris will, no need to ask," Marion laughed.

"Where would they be, Mrs. Manning?"

"The projection room, dear, two doors from the office. It's been closed up. That's probably why you haven't noticed it."

Adrienne went in search of the menfolk. The film had obviously been shown. There they were leaning against the desk smoking and talking. Grant appeared to be pressing home a point and Chris was nodding his head vigorously.

"Excuse me, gentlemen," she put in.

"Adrienne, my love, you've grown desperate for my company." Chris came away from the table and took her hand, pressing it against his heart.

She looked up at him smilingly. "Well, that, and are you desperate for some supper?"

"Ye gods, yes. It's an age since I've eaten. Come on, Grant, let's go to it."

"We won't disturb Mrs. Ford, Chris. Give your mother a shock and make the coffee. I'll show Adrienne around here. She hasn't seen it."

"Your wish is my command."

"Oh, Chris" – Grant detained him – "on second' thoughts you'd better get Marion to make it. We have to drink it, after all."

"Well said, sir." Chris disappeared around the door saying, "Shaken but not stirred."

"Come in, Adrienne. You look posed for flight."

"Not at all, Mr. Manning. I'm quite interested."

"Call me Mr. Manning again, my girl, and you'll regret it!" The grey eyes gave fair warning.

"Yes, sir." Adrienne spoke involuntarily and then caught her bottom lip with her small white teeth. "Yes, Grant," she smiled up at him, and wished she hadn't, for his eyes grew bright and challenging. She turned away from them. "Inner sanctum?" she queried.

Grant laughed. "A remark suitable to your age group! No, my dear, the projection room. There's a lot of valuable film here on projects and places and various techniques. You won't need to worry about it. I really wanted to speak to you about Chris."

Adrienne controlled an impulse to run.

"You can't run away, child. Your eyes are straight from the woodland." Grant leant back against the desk. "Please don't encourage him, Adrienne." He stayed her with one hand. "You do, you may not know it, but you do. It's in your eyes and your voice and even the curve of your mouth."

Adrienne shut her eyes and when she opened them they were quite brilliant with denial. "Mr. Manning!" He pulled her towards him and his grip was painful. "Grant," she protested, "I really don't know what to say. I don't encourage Chris, you must know that. In any case, it's quite unfair, if I could care for Chris . . ."

"But you couldn't, Adrienne. Not the way he's beginning to care for you. You know it and I know it." He took the hand that he had hurt and began to stroke the fine network of veins on the inside of her wrist.

Adrienne shivered. "Oh, stop, Grant!" She pulled her hand away. "I'm beginning to feel like a hypnotised rabbit. I think I'll go back to Sydney."

Grant laughed at that. "Just remember, my dear, Chris is a fine boy, but he needs someone far less complex than you." He reached over her head and turned off the light. "Come and have coffee."

It was Sunday midday before Adrienne saw Grant and Chris and the week-end had almost gone. She felt a little saddened. Chris was so nice. It was a pity really that he seemed to like her. She didn't want to be the one to hurt him, but he was so likeable it was difficult not to show his liking was returned. Surely he couldn't read anything more into it? She went through to the cool of the veranda where Mrs. Manning and Marion were discussing means of raising money for the hospital annexe.

"Why not a barbecue?" Adrienne suggested. "Charge everyone a dollar, or even two or three, seeing it's such a good cause and will ultimately benefit everyone." She smiled at the other two.

"A barbecue, dear?" Mrs. Manning's interest was aroused, but only slightly. She was not one for the great outdoors.

"Why not, Helen? I think it's a good idea." Marion sat forward. "The grounds would be marvellous. No need for a crowd in the house. I could just see them loose among the treasures." Her voice was affectionate but a little dry. Saranga Homestead was a byword in the State.

Adrienne was enthusiastic. "We could string coloured lights and lanterns among the trees. I can just see it!"

"Coloured lights, dear?" Mrs. Manning obviously couldn't.

"Come on, now Helen, it will only be temporary," Marion laughed. "We could raise a lot of money."

That settled it. Mrs. Manning was out to raise money. "When do you think we should have it?" she queried.

"Oh, I think a fortnight is plenty of notice. Not that anyone's going anywhere." Marion was quietly amused. One day dawned pretty much like another out West.

Mrs. Manning's eyes took on the look of a born planner. "I'll speak to Grant at lunchtime. There's not a moment to lose."

Adrienne caught Marion's eye and they both diverted their attentions to the almond tree. Mrs. Manning could be very funny sometimes when she least intended to be. Under their eyes she had assumed the mantle of first lady of the district.

At lunch Grant amusedly consented to having Saranga turned into one big barbecue area. "Adrienne's idea, I suppose," he queried with a maddening quirk to his mouth. Adrienne wouldn't look at him.

Marion and Chris left early in the afternoon. They couldn't afford to be away from Careewa for long, although they had a most reliable leading hand. They all walked out to the car and Chris fell behind to speak to Adrienne.

"Did you miss me today?" he wanted to know.

"What time today, Chris?" Adrienne looked up at him and laughed.

"Don't evade the question. I've hardly seen you. Grant had me down with the Moreton stock all morning."

"Come on, Chris, your mother is waiting," Grant called lazily from the car.

"Oh, damn! We'll go over to Donaldsons' one day when I've got a bit of time," he promised.

"That will be nice, Chris, and thank you once more for my picnic. It really was the nicest I've ever been on."

"You've made my day, girl." Chris grinned down at her.

"I mean it, Chris." Wasn't it true? – and to blazes with Mr. Manning!

They reached the others and Chris swung behind the wheel with a final wave to them all.

"See you soon, Helen," Marion called. "You too, Adrienne, my dear. You're always welcome over at Careewa." She released Grant's hand and he stood away from the car.

"Take her away, Chris." He nodded to his cousin and they watched until the station wagon had cleared the bend in the drive.

"One thing's certain," Mrs. Manning remarked as they walked back to the house, "it will be a lot quieter without Chris."

CHAPTER FIVE

MANY times in the next fortnight Adrienne had cause to regret ever mentioning a barbecue. She now found herself going non-stop. Not only was there Grant's work to be attended to, but she was becoming daily more indispensable to Mrs. Manning. The days went past in a whirl and, even with Mrs. Ford's cooking, she was noticeably losing weight.

"I'll be glad when this barbecue is over," Grant remarked one morning as he was signing the mail.

"Me too," Adrienne found herself agreeing without even realising it.

He looked down at her, the fine bones of her face a shade more prominent, and for once his eyes weren't mocking. "Let me know if it's too much for you. Helen sometimes gets carried away with her good deeds. You're definitely thinner." Adrienne blinked and he laughed at her. "Didn't you think I'd notice?" The grey eyes were appraising. "Oh, I do, Adrienne, I do." He bundled the letters together and passed them across to her. "Helen wants those lanterns and whatnots installed. You'd better come in with me later this afternoon."

He must have taken her consent for granted because he turned and walked out of the office without another word. Adrienne returned to the typing with renewed vigour. She had something to look forward to. She bent her head and her fingers flew. So he had noticed all the extra hours she had put in with Mrs. Manning! When he wasn't being very much beyond her, he was very nice.

The afternoon couldn't come quickly enough. About two-thirty Grant put Adrienne into the front seat of the Mercedes and waved a nonchalant hand to Mrs. Manning, who had come out on to the veranda with final instructions.

"Relax, child. You're on the edge of the seat." Adrienne sank back into the plush upholstery and prepared to enjoy the drive. They swept around the bend in the road and Grant asked casually, "What made you leave home, Adrienne? Your wicked stepmother?" He was too clever by half!

"Not so wicked. She just didn't want me around, but she loves my father, so I suppose that's all that matters. I was in the way."

He absorbed this piece of information, then asked quietly, "How long ago did you lose your mother?"

"Ten years almost to the day. I remember I'd won a medal for a music exam and I couldn't wait to go up and tell her. She was in hospital, you see. I never saw her and she never knew about it. Don't ask me any more, Grant." Her voice sank.

The grey eyes he turned to her were almost as gentle as Marion's. "You can cry with me, little one. A salutory cry won't hurt you. I don't imagine you've done much of it." His voice somehow had the effect of sobering her, but she avoided any further reference to her mother.

Grant let a few miles go past, then he mused aloud, "How would you go about transplanting an orchid?"

Adrienne turned to him, a little surprised at the question. She had not thought him interested in such things. "I don't know, Grant, but I should think you would be able to find out easily enough."

"You've no vanity, have you? I was referring to you."

Adrienne coloured a little at the remark and answered on a reflex action. "Chris asked me the same thing, but he didn't express himself quite so extravagantly."

"Did he now?" He spoke as if his mind was already somewhere else. Adrienne, glancing at the chiselled profile, found it remote. The change in him was disconcerting to say the least. She sank back against the upholstery. They drove into the town in silence and Grant parked outside the Memorial Hall.

"Is there anything you want while we're here?"

"Oh yes," she said urgently. "Talcum powder."

"Not really?" The very white teeh flashed as he handed her out. "*Voilà*! The chemist!" He pointed across the street, then flicked back his cuff. "I've got a few things to attend to. Take your time, but be back here in twenty-five minutes."

Adrienne narrowed her eyes against the sun and crossed to the other side of the street. She might as well have a good look around while she was here. Her presence did not go unnoticed. She could feel the eyes on her and recognised a few faces from the Hospital Committee Meeting. She smiled whenever someone chanced to smile at her, which was often. It was something of a novelty when she remembered the sights that paraded up and down the streets of Sydney without even turning a head.

Adrienne made a few purchases at the chemist shop and bought a new lipstick while she was at it. There was an extraordinary thing about lipstick – you could be made up to the nines otherwise, but if you weren't wearing lipstick you just weren't wearing make-up, according to a man. She thought of her father with affection. Many was the time she had come to the dinner table minus lipstick but fully made-up otherwise, and her father had turned to her with a "cutting it fine, aren't you?" preparatory to an evening out. She smiled to herself and caught the sales girl's curious look.

She thanked her and walked out into the sunshine. A piece of tissue paper blew across her path and landed in the gutter. Adrienne watched it idly. It was a pretty pink shade like from a shoe box, and then her eyes brightened. "That's it, tissue paper!" Mrs. Manning intended to have tables set up in the grounds for the barbecue covered with checked gingham of varying colours. Why not giant tissue paper flowers of the same colour as the tablecloths? Real flowers in this instance would be inappropriate, but these would be just the thing. Her enthusiasm mounted. She was essentially a creature of impulse, but her enthusiasm was brought up with a jolt. Why did she always come out with only a few dollars in her purse? She had nearly spent that. The paper itself was nothing, but she would need staples, a stapler, wooden dowels, thin wire and some rubber cement. Adrienne was so carried away with her idea that she went in search of Grant.

The first place she tried was the pastoral agency. He had been there, but was probably at the bank at the moment. Adrienne hurried across to the air-conditioned bank and walked straight up to Grant. "Oh, Grant, I have an idea!" she announced.

"Not here, dear," the grey eyes glimmered with amusement.

"Please be serious, Grant."

"Why shouldn't I be?" he grinned, and then assumed some gravity. "What is it, Adrienne?"

"I want to make some paper flowers for the barbecue."

"Good grief, aren't there enough real flowers at Saranga?" He was definitely at sea.

"These are quite different, Grant, and very effective," she explained patiently. "The women could take them home if they liked. Not everyone has your gardens, you know."

"I stand reproved, Miss Brent. Well, what about these paper flowers?"

"I haven't enough money with me to buy all the things I need."

"Good gracious!"

"Oh, please be serious, Grant."

He nodded pleasantly to the bank clerk who came over to him with some papers, then took Adrienne by the elbow and ushered her out on to the street. "Right, I'm serious. Lead the way."

"I don't know where the hardware store is, Grant." She looked up at him, her eyes widening.

He crossed to her outside. "Well, it seems I lead the way." They walked on for about a hundred yards, then Grant came to an exaggerated halt, pointing theatrically – "The hardware store, Adrienne."

They went in and Adrienne made her various purchases while the young assistant stared avidly from one to the other.

"Anything up, Tom?" Grant addressed the boy.

"No, sir, of course not." Tom started to fidget with his account book.

"How's the family?" Grant went on. "Your father back yet?"

Tom hastened to give all the news of home.

"You made him nervous," Adrienne remarked when they were out on the footpath once more.

"Not so nervous that he couldn't control his curiosity." Grant looked down at his watch. "What next?"

"I'll just get the tissue paper, then I'm finished." She sounded quite apologetic.

"Come along then, little one, this is something new for me."

Ten minutes later they were on the road for Saranga. Grant slanted her an indulgent glance. "Haven't you got enough to do?"

"I'll enjoy doing this. They'll look lovely on the tables. Just wait and see."

Grant laughed in genuine amusement. "What a remarkable child you are! Is there no end to your talents?"

"I can't yodel like Chris."

Grant changed gear rather forcibly for him. "So we're back to Chris again?"

The miles flew past and Adrienne gazed abstractedly through the window, her mind on colour combination. "Oh, please stop, Grant. This is my lucky day."

"Great heavens!" He pulled the car up on the side of the road and turned on her in mock exasperation.

"You won't believe this, Grant, but that's a tortured

92

willow over there." She pointed to a tree a few feet off the road.

Grant touched his forehead fleetingly, then looked up at the roof of the car. "Some would forgive me for not believing it. You're not another little Emily Dickinson, are you?"

Adrienne hadn't heard him. She was out of the car and moving towards the tree. Grant looked straight ahead of him for a few seconds then he laughed to himself and got out of the car. He crossed over to where Adrienne appeared to be embracing some branches and he started to whistle loudly and tunelessly.

Adrienne turned to him with shining eyes. "Oh, Grant, this is a find! Don't you see? After you strip the bark these branches make wonderful floral arrangements. We'll just have to find the right branches, that's all."

Grant feigned relief. "Is that all? I was preparing myself for Desdemona's aria. You don't sing, by any chance?" His smile was sharply satirical.

Adrienne laughed and pointed to some branches. "That one, Grant, and this one here, and these two, I think."

He broke off the weird-looking branches according to her instructions, then took them back to the boot of the car. With the hundred and one things he had to get through today, here he was collecting floral arrangements! "Don't for heaven's sake ever tell me there are fairies at the bottom of Saranga, or I might find myself looking for them," he remarked very blandly.

"You won't think it so silly when you see the results, Grant, I assure you." Adrienne patted the branches lovingly. "Next thing you know you'll be commissioning me for an arrangement for Vera."

He met her brilliant dark gaze and straightened up, then gave the hand resting on the boot of the car a hard slap. "That's for being cheeky! Back in the car!"

Mrs. Manning at least was extremely interested in

Adrienne's ideas. The two women discussed them interminably over dinner. After a particularly involved bit of women's talk, Adrienne turned to the silent Grant with a query, "Have we a big copper about the place?"

"Heavens!" he uttered violently, and pushed back his chair. He took in the two faces looking up at him with some awe and started to laugh. "I suppose on reflection you could mean some sort of vat, dear child." He picked up his coffee, bent on having it in peace. "I've been brainwashed into thinking you wanted some member of the constabulary to act as a piece of decor. It's taken a moment to assimilate it."

"Oh, Grant!" Adrienne relaxed. He had looked thoroughly alarming for a while there.

The light eyes were still amused. "You answer our little homemaker, Helen. This is out of my line."

"You're leaving us, then, Grant?" Mrs. Manning's voice trailed upwards in surprise.

"Yes, dear lady. I must regretfully leave you to your Home and Garden session."

They watched the broad back retreating in a disbelieving silence. "I do believe we got on his nerves." Mrs. Manning spoke with the utmost wonder.

Adrienne looked back at her without really seeing her, then she broke into a peal of laughter. "A big copper!" she gasped, and to Mrs. Manning's astonishment pushed back her chair and tore from the room.

The hostess of the evening was staggered to find herself taking coffee alone.

Adrienne looked up from the typewriter with a smile when Grant came into the office next morning. He watched her thoughtfully. The morning sun slanted across the office and spilled over the thick shiny hair and the corn silk blouse, the bare arms a smooth pale gold.

Adrienne's voice lifted hesitantly. "Grant." He had

been silent for so long with a rather curious expression on his still face.

His expression sharpened and became vital. "What are you looking so well and rested for, young woman? Helen tells me you were up until after midnight making those confounded flowers."

"I was. Do you want to see them?" She rose to her feet eagerly.

"Adrienne," the narrowed eyes were half-smiling. "Whenever I'm with you I feel like a net has been flung over my head and I'm enmeshed in it. Will you stop diverting me!" She sat down reproved and looked at the typewriter. Grant smiled. "Of course I want to see the flowers, child. All in good time." He came round the desk and put down a pile of closely written foolscap pages in front of her. "Check this over before you type it. You'll have to paragraph it, etc. I've just gone straight through. As you'll see, it's an article on wool promotion for the International Secretariat. We've some very stiff competition from synthetics, I can tell you. They spend a great deal more on promotion."

Adrienne nodded, her mind already on it.

"That and the mail should take you until lunchtime. You can do those blessed flowers this afternoon." She looked up at him quickly and he glinted back at her, "Don't protest too much or I'll change my mind."

She leaned back in her chair. "I sit here speechless with gratitude."

His mouth twitched. "Get on with it, Lorelei. I'll be back late this evening. I told Helen not to wait dinner." He moved to the door with his long stride. "So long, little one."

Adrienne worked the whole morning on the article and missed lunch to catch up on the mail. Afterwards she went through to her room to collect all her paraphernalia and took it through to the office. Mrs. Manning had been quite lyrical when she had seen the results of her night's work and that was before breakfast too. Already she'd thought of some more places where they could put the blessed things.

Adrienne bent over her colourful array. They were extraordinarily effective and for so little cost. The huge full-blown roses were her speciality. Seeing they were quite obviously artificial, Adrienne didn't limit herself with her colour schemes. She alternated blues and mauves, pinks and crimsons, yellows and pinks in the petal arrangements according to the snippets of material Mrs. Manning had given her.

She was just cutting out some more shapes when Mrs. Manning appeared at the doorway, one hand to her head. "Oh, do come, Adrienne dear, and help me decide where these lights and things should go." Adrienne put down the scissors and followed her out into the drive.

A wry little man with the face of one of the not so wise monkeys touched his hat to Adrienne, then transferred his gaze to Mrs. Manning. That lady herself was busy outlining her ideas to Adrienne. She was being extremely articulate and numerous hand gestures accompanied the flow of words. The little visitor was looking at her with patent disbelief. He had heard about Mrs. Manning, but he had never met her. Certainly she was nothing like any of his womenfolk. Adrienne repressed a smile at the transparency of his expression. No doubt he would turn to her with the very same look. She could be equally voluble on occasions and used her hand to illustrate a point perhaps even more so. She concentrated on a plan of lighting while the little man skimmed up and down trees with uncanny agility.

"I think we've found the missing link?" Adrienne whispered in a soft voice.

"Oh, please, dear, I'll have to go into the house." Mrs. Manning controlled her face with an effort and spoke graciously to the diminutive electrician.

Even if she did have a fantastic lot to say for herself she was a lady, he thought, with utter fairness.

96

It took almost two hours, however, before he was through, and Adrienne found she had developed a violent headache and the sun beat down heavy and hot.

"It's the sun, dear. You wouldn't be used to it so far inland. Go in and lie down for an hour."

Adrienne put her hand to her temple where a little devil was hammering away industriously. "I think I'll have to, Mrs. Manning. It couldn't be migraine, I haven't had that for at least four years."

Mrs. Manning turned to her with concern. "Come back into the house, Adrienne. You're pale." They walked up to the cool of the veranda and through to the hall. "Just wait a moment, dear, and I'll get you some of my Vega-nin." Mrs. Manning hurried out of the room and came back with a glass of water and two tablets. "Take those and lie down. I've been working you too hard. Grant told me I had."

"Not at all, Mrs. Manning. The sun is very strong out here." Adrienne turned towards the door. "Don't worry, these will do the trick."

"I hope so, dear. I think I'll follow my own advice and have a rest too. I'm not as young as I think I am." She laughed a little and disappeared with a wave of her hand.

When she was in her room, Adrienne drew the blinds and turned down the bedspread. Her head was pounding. She swallowed the tablets and lay back. An hour's rest should help. She closed her eyes thankfully and sank into the foam rubber pillow.

The sun had gone down before she opened her eyes, and she gazed up at the blinds in consternation. Surely it couldn't be that late. She checked her watch – it was six o'clock. Well, at least her headache had gone. She splashed her face half a dozen times with cold water, ran a comb through her hair, and left it swinging loose. Fresh lipstick and she felt a lot brighter, but how on earth was she going to fit in all the things she had to do?

At dinner Mrs. Manning was relieved to see her looking

so much better. "I fully intend giving you a hand with those flowers." She was wearing her most determined expression. "There must be something I can do."

"Well, you could cut out the shapes if you like and I'll trim them." Adrienne laughed. "it's not very rewarding, you may get bored."

"Bored or not, I intend to try." Mrs. Manning turned her attention to the brandied peaches.

True to her word, she did try, but was interrupted so many times by calls from committee members that Adrienne found she would have worked much faster on her own. As it was, she was waiting on Mrs. Manning for the petals. About nine-thirty Adrienne brought coffee through for the two of them while Mrs. Manning unsuccessfully tried to conceal a yawn.

"I'm afraid I've not been much use to you, dear." She looked down at the improbable flowers blooming in her living room. "You'll be besieged with enquiries on how to make them, you know. They're quite amazingly attractive."

Adrienne held up an American Beauty rose fully six inches in diameter and bent her head over it. "I'm ready for pictures."

Mrs. Manning sat up. "Pictures! Of course! You would be ideal for a poster." Her eyes flickered with a moment's concentration.

Adrienne's smile faded. "Oh, please, Mrs. Manning, I couldn't bear that."

Mrs. Manning sank back. "No, I suppose not, dear – this barbecue has me mad." She put her cup and saucer down and pushed up from the chair. "You'll have to excuse me, Adrienne. I've absolutely had it." She smiled down at the girl. "Don't sit up here too long. We've a few hectic days in front of us."

She said goodnight and left Adrienne to the quiet of the house. A profusion of flowers grew under her hands. She cut and trimmed and twisted, secured her blooms and laid

98

them carefully around her. Another two dozen and she would call it a night. She worked on for a while, then rested her head back and blinked rapidly a few times to refresh her eyes. When she lifted her head her eyes fell on the drink cabinet, and she thought, The very thing! A brandy should do it. It was supposed to be a stimulant and that was what she needed. She got up and went over to investigate. What a formidable array! She picked on a bottle which looked like Marie Bressard. She poured a nip or two, she wasn't sure, and took it back to the centre of the room. She slipped down on a cushion and tried it. Ye gods, it was not to her taste. She gulped it down. It should be a stimulant with a taste like that!

When Grant let himself into the house soon after eleven he found the living room a blaze of lights, and wondering who was still up, he strode towards the room and stopped on the threshold. Adrienne lay like a flower among her creations, her head on a crimson cushion. He switched off the chandelier, leaving only the soft wall lighting and walked towards her. He slipped an arm underneath her and she awoke with a start, her eyes huge and bemused.

"Grant, are you home?" she whispered.

He didn't reply but swung her up into his arms, and quite unselfconsciously she put her own around his neck.

"Have you been raiding my brandy?" The smile in his voice brought a delicate flush of colour to her face. He held her as easily as a child and didn't seem inclined to put her down.

"This isn't very businesslike, Grant," she murmured.

The grey eyes mocked her. "But then we've never had a very businesslike arrangement, have we, Miss Brent?" The lazy eyes took on a glitter and Adrienne turned her face into her hand. "What are you doing?" He held her higher in his arms and bent closer to her.

Adrienne's colour mounted. "I thought you were going to kiss me. Don't ask me why."

There was a startled silence and Grant smothered a

laugh. "Kissing one's secretary is one way of asking for trouble, little one. In any case, I don't kiss babies, except perhaps like this . . ." He brushed his mouth lightly up and down under her ear, and a shiver of excitement shot through her. The feel of his mouth on her skin was almost too much for her. For a baby kiss it was having rather a devastating effect.

"Please put me down, Grant," she managed.

For a moment he seemed on the point of refusing her request, then he lowered her gently to her feet. Adrienne turned and went to tidy up her night's work.

"That can wait until morning. You'd better take yourself off now," he added dangerously.

Adrienne bade him a hasty goodnight.

CHAPTER SIX

THE days before the barbecue slipped by with rapidity. Over two hundred people were expected, and the bulk of the organisation fell squarely on the shoulders of Mrs. Manning as hostess. She in turn delegated a great many tasks to the willing and highly competent Adrienne. As Mrs. Manning remarked to Grant one morning before breakfast, "I don't see how I could possibly manage without her." With all due modesty, Adrienne had wondered the same thing.

Not that Marion didn't come in for her share of the work. She was frequently in and out of Saranga, though Chris seemed to be more than usually busy. Grant certainly was. He was in the process of negotiating the sale of his crack stallion, Mountain Gold. All in all, very little was seen of the menfolk.

The Saturday morning of the barbecue dawned bright and cloudless. It was perfect weather for a barbecue, if a storm didn't come. One could never be absolutely sure. All that remained to be done was the placing of the flowers, which could be done before lunch. The food and the delectable accompaniments to the steaks had long since been organised. It was just as well because Mrs. Manning and her young helper had nearly exhausted themselves.

After lunch Adrienne went out into the grounds to check over all she had done in the morning with Marion's invaluable help. She was just wending her way through the tables, when Grant came down from the house.

"Adrienne!"

She leant against the long trellis and waited for him to come up to her. Under the trees it was deliciously cool, though her dress still stuck to her back. "Yes, Grant?" She lifted her eyes to the lean bronzed face. It seemed ages since they had had one relaxed moment together.

He was silent for a moment, taking in her slight pallor, then he leant back against the trellis, running his hand over the tablecloth. "Go inside, and lie down before you fall down. Helen is resting – you do the same. The whole thing has been too much for you. There are other women, Helen should utilise their services more." Mrs. Manning was coming in for a little criticism. Unthinkingly she rested against him for a moment and he put his arm around her and walked her back to the house. "You seem more than usually tiny." He glanced down in mild surprise. As it was she barely reached his shoulder.

"No heels on my sandals, I suppose," Adrienne explained naively. They both looked down at the thin leather straps that criss-crossed her narrow foot and passed as sandals.

"What lovely limbs you've got," Grant spoke almost absentmindedly.

Adrienne looked no higher than the cleft chin. "You are being nice today, Grant. It must be the party spirit."

The arm across her back tightened slightly. "And the party hasn't started yet," he emphasised, the tone of his voice reducing her bones to jelly. She couldn't for the life of her think of an appropriate reply, so she wisely said nothing. They reached the house and Grant looked down at her, issuing an order at the same time. "Rest until about six. You have plenty of time." He turned her towards her room and made for the office. He at least was inexhaustible!

Adrienne slipped into a housecoat and lay down. She knew she couldn't possibly sleep, the promptly did just that. The grandfather clock in the hall chimed five-thirty before she woke suddenly and completely. Why not have a leisurely bath instead of her usual shower? She ran the bath, filling it nearly to the top, and sprinkled the water extravagantly with expensive bath salts. They had been a birthday present. She would never have bought them for herself. The steam rose fragrant and gardenia-scented.

What luxury! She bathed without haste, then dusted herself down with the matching talc, slipping back into her housecoat to make up.

Thank goodness the colour had come back into her face, she considered. She had been looking a little pale on it. Adrienne applied her all-in-one foundation with a light expert hand and proceeded to darken her already dark eyelashes, adding the faintest whisper of gold frosted green eye-shadow. She outlined her mouth with a brush, then filled in with the new lipstick, an iridescent pinky beige bearing the improbable name of Desert Sand.

She had decided to wear her hair pulled back from her face and arranged in a smooth shining bell at the back. It seemed to suit her outfit. Her earrings too would show to better advantage. They were right in vogue, long and dangly in beaten gold, and no one would guess they had belonged to her grandmother. Adrienne had inherited all her grandmother's "pieces", as she used to call them, and treasured them dearly. Neither were they left to languish in their rusty black velvet box, but were taken out and given a wearing. In fact, Adrienne's gift of physical beauty carried the heavy old-fashioned jewellery to perfection.

She screwed on the earrings and watched them swing. They were definitely "in". They pointed up her vivid beauty and threw a gleam across her high cheek bones.

She turned away from the mirror and went to the wardrobe. Now for her dress. She slipped into it quickly. It was a black silk shimmer with splashes of brown and gold. She adjusted the shoestring straps and wriggled into the fitted bra top. The zipper checked at the back, not that there was much back, and she let it go at that.

The house looked gay and festive and she found her step quickening. The giant auratum lilies in the hallway were a stroke of genius. Adrienne gazed down at them with pleasure. They caught and held your attention in their glowing copper tubs. She had persuaded Grant to bring them into the hallway for the occasion, and they made a

103

magnificent interior decoration. The flowers were nearly nine inches across of deepest crimson, yellow-rayed and speckled with white. The perfume was superb, a touch of the exotic. The lilies might have had their home in Asia, but they grew many times larger and more beautiful in Australia. But she couldn't stand there lost in admiration. Mrs. Manning would be bound to have something for her to do.

There she was, talking to Grant – Grant impossibly handsome in biscuit-coloured slacks and a matching Italian knit.

Mrs. Manning's face lit up when she saw her young helper, but Grant's black eyebrows came together in a frown. "You'll have to change that, Adrienne," he said.

"Whatever do you mean, Grant? Adrienne looks lovely." Mrs. Manning was simply astonished.

"It's not suitable, that's all." The lean jaw tightened.

Adrienne felt deeply mortified. The hot colour swept into her face and she turned and fled, but not before they saw the quick tears spring to her eyes.

"How could you, Grant, and so unlike you!" Mrs. Manning was upset. "She looked simply stunning."

"That's just it," he clipped out. "The whole district will be here tonight, and they'll be staring enough as it is."

His aunt blinked once or twice, and sighed deeply. "Well, I'd better go to her, poor girl. You've hurt her feelings, and no wonder. She's been so good too." She turned to go, but Grant stayed her with one hand.

"Don't worry, Helen, I'll go. You'd better give everything a final check."

Mrs. Manning acquiesced, not altogether happily, but went through to the kitchen for a last consultation with Mrs. Ford.

Grant rapped quietly on Adrienne's door. "Are you there, Adrienne? I'd like to speak to you." There was a complete silence from the other side of the door. "Open the door, Adrienne!" He was greeted by more silence. His tone hardened. "I hope this door isn't locked, Adrienne, because I'm coming in."

The door flung to and he saw her sitting disconsolately on the side of the bed. Her shiny head was bent and one strap had slipped off her shoulder.

"Adrienne." She refused to acknowledge his presence. He walked over to the bed and sat down beside her. Adrienne turned her head determinedly away from him. "Look here, child, I'm sorry I was so curt just now. I didn't mean to be. It was just . . . you look very well, you know that, but that dress . . . it's too damned provocative."

There was a scarcely perceptible movement of her head and he ran a slow finger down the length of her spine. She trembled violently. "Do you see what I mean?"

Adrienne was shocked into looking at him. "I don't imagine anyone will be doing that."

"Well, you don't know, do you?" he answered lightly.

She looked down at her lap again and the tears threatened. "You embarrassed me and made me feel badly dressed, and I'm sure I hate you!"

"Come now." Grant drew her to her feet. "It's not as bad as that. There'll be a lot of people here tonight and I want you covered." He tilted her chin up towards him. "Wear that dress you had on the other night. It's pretty." Her soft mouth quivered and he shook her slightly. "Come on now, Adrienne. I'm a tactless brute, but I didn't mean to hurt you." He let go of her and turned to the door. "Hurry up now, Helen will be needing you."

When he had gone Adrienne went to the wardrobe and took out the cream voile.

The barbecue was well and truly swinging by half-past seven. The grounds were swarming with laughing, chattering people and their numerous offspring; and the drive was brilliant with a hundred car beams. Adrienne saw women in every conceivable form of casual dress. There were even shorts present.

"The damned cheek of him!" she fumed. She had caught sight of Vera in a patio dress that was every bit as bare as her skimmer, probably more so – in fact, a lot more of Vera was showing.

In another half hour the fires were ablaze and the party in full swing. Adrienne found that she had little time to enjoy it because the food was disappearing at a phenomenal rate. For once Mrs. Ford welcomed a hand.

"See those bottles of pickled onions and gherkins, get those down and into dishes. Oh yes, the olives too." She spoke in great haste and turned back to arranging more salad on a huge platter.

Adrienne did as she was told and carried the piled-up dishes out to the tables. The mustard and relish were going down, so she went back for more. The youngsters were eating that; she had seen them at it.

By half-past eight she still hadn't had a bite to eat. There was Vera always eating, it seemed, and never offering a helping hand. Marion too had not eaten and Mrs. Manning was deep in conversation with a terrifying old lady in a blue silk trouser suit, her hair the most outlandish and improbable shade of pink. Adrienne found out afterwards that she was one of the wealthiest women in Australia and a "character". She certainly dressed the part.

She was just replacing a huge mixed salad when Vera stopped her. "Rather thick on the ground, aren't we?" the other girl drawled and much as she disliked her, Adrienne laughed. Vera helped herself to a sizeable portion of salad and topped it liberally with mayonnaise. At that precise moment the Donaldson's youngest, a sturdy little chap of about five, careered into the two girls and hurled some of the dressing over the front of Vera's Pucci creation.

"You grubby little beast!" she jerked out violently, and caught him by the shoulder. His tiny mouth fell open. The lady looked ready to eat him. "Oh, heavens, just look at

106

me!" Vera was nearly incoherent with rage. She gave the child a small push and the short brown legs went from under him – he went sprawling. To his great credit he didn't cry. Adrienne sprang forward and set him on his feet.

"That was funny, little man," she smiled into the apprehensive young face. "You tipped up!" He kept his eyes trained on the smiling face and wouldn't look at Vera. "Hop off now to Mummy." She gave him a pat and a final dust down and sent him on his way. "You bitch!" she burst out.

"I beg your pardon?" Vera exploded in incredulous indignation.

"You heard what I said, and that's what you are," Adrienne replied very firmly indeed.

Vera's face worked. "You wait until Grant hears about this!"

"Until Grant hears about what?" The cool grey eyes travelled from Adrienne, still kneeling, to the white-faced Vera. He crossed over and gave Adrienne his hand. She hopped up lightly and for a moment it seemed as though they were ranged together.

"Oh, nothing serious, darling." Vera sounded quite tearful. "Miss Brent never misses an opportunity to be rude to me, that's all." She put up a hand to flick away an imaginary tear. "Perhaps you could make her apologise."

Grant's hand came down heavily on Adrienne's shoulder. "Adrienne, apologise to Vera for calling her a bitch," he said smoothly.

Both girls started. So he had heard. Adrienne thought, but had probably seen nothing. She stiffened under his hand, but he kept it there. She remained conspicuously silent. "I'll be blowed if I will!" she fumed inwardly.

"Adrienne," the pressure increased.

"I do apologise for calling you a bitch, Miss Sterling," she said, and for her own satisfaction made it sound as

107

though there were far more suitable words she had regretfully missed.

Grant's hand fell to his side and he crossed to the mollified Vera.

"The girl must be stupid! Did she really think that was an apology?"

"Don't let's spoil a pleasant evening, girls," Grant chided, and steered Vera back into the throng without even a backward glance at his secretary.

Later on when Chris brought over a plate heaped high with food, Adrienne found she was so churned up she couldn't eat a bit of it.

"How I'd love to stay with you, sweetheart, but I must go back," Chris groaned. Nevertheless he did stay for a few minutes, talking, then returned to duty behind the makeshift bar. He certainly had a calming effect.

Later in the evening Tammy wandered up and sat down beside Adrienne. "Rory's been telling me about the pretty lady. I knew it wasn't Vera. She's a bitch if ever there was one." Evidently they were in complete agreement over Vera. Tammy leaned back, the coloured lights flickering over her troubled young face. "I know it's cheek, Adrienne, but I feel I can ask you." She turned suddenly. "What do you think of Chris?"

Adrienne had been expecting the question, so she smiled back into the anxious eyes. "I *like* him very much, Tammy," she stressed, "if that's what you mean."

"That's what I do mean, and I'm glad." She drew in her lip. "You see, I want him. Crazy, isn't it? He doesn't even see me. Not while you're around anyway," she added dejectedly. "You've got something" . . . she groped for a word and came up with the one she thought appropriate . . . "mysterious."

Adrienne burst out laughing. "Oh, heavens, Tammy, not mysterious!" There was at least one person who could read her like a book.

"Yes, mysterious," Tammy persisted. "Like that

Mona Lisa." She turned impatiently on Adrienne, who was much amused and rather touched.

"Mona Lisa indeed!" She hoped she didn't smirk like that.

"You'd know what I meant if you could see yourself."

Adrienne sobered quickly. Tammy sounded very dispirited. "Well, look, Tammy, perhaps you could change your style with Chris. He looks on you as part of his childhood, the proverbial girl next door. Maybe you should be a bit more . . . er . . . mysterious, for want of a better word." She resisted an impulse to laugh.

Tammy was interested.

"Do you think it would work?" she asked.

Frankly, Adrienne had no idea, but she thought it was worth a try. "Wear a pretty dress when Chris comes instead of jeans and a shirt. Not that you don't look nice in them, Tammy, you do." Tammy was wearing just that. "It's only that I don't think there's a man alive who doesn't prefer a dress to slacks on a woman. You could wear a little more make-up too, Tammy, there's nothing like it. All we need's a little camouflage." Tammy used the briefest rub of lipstick and little else. Her eyes definitely needed definition. Adrienne elaborated a little for the other girl's benefit.

Tammy looked at the now wholly serious Adrienne. "Well, I'll say this for you, you don't have any tickets on yourself. I've known lots of girls not half as pretty as you, who thought they were just marvellous."

"Looks don't mean everything, Tam, but they certainly help. Chris needs someone like you. It's up to you to show him just how much. Use some feminine wiles on him, fascinate him." She wanted to laugh again.

Tammy did. "You're nice," she gurgled.

"The conflicting statements one hears in the space of an evening!" Grant had come up behind them and Tammy swivelled round to speak to him.

"Hallo, Mr. Manning," she said brightly. "It's a super

evening. The committee should make a fortune." She jumped up to give him her place. "I'll remember what you said, Adrienne." She waved gaily and disappeared into the crowd.

"What did you say, Adrienne?" Grant inquired lazily.

"I don't think you would be interested, would you?" Adrienne answered a shade crossly, and went to get up.

He drew her back firmly. "Sit still, little one. I've just been talking to our millionairess and I need respite."

"I know. I saw you," Adrienne remarked with sarcasm. "You looked like she was quite the most interesting woman you had spoken to all evening."

Grant laughed. "Well, she is a character. I must introduce you."

Adrienne shifted uneasily. That was an honour she could afford to let pass. "What else shall we talk about? The rare fashions here tonight. There are some you'll notice."

Grant was amused. "They don't look the same," he observed drily. A group of excited youngsters careered around the drive quite out of parental control. Grant stood up and held out a hand. "Come down to the lily pond. It's less hectic there."

Adrienne took his outstretched hand and walked beside him out of the circle of light. "I haven't seen Mrs. Manning for some time," she remarked.

"She's lying down for a while, having done her duty. This sort of thing is not really her style."

"Oh, dear heaven!" Adrienne's blood froze.

"What is it?" He turned her to him swiftly, his voice urgent.

She shuddered and her voice wavered precariously. "A frog jumped over my foot."

He let go of her in amazement. "A frog jumped over your foot!" He said it quite blankly, then repeated it, spacing the words the better to comprehend it.

Adrienne flung away from him violently. "I hate frogs,

110

I hate you, and I've had a perfectly hateful evening!"

Grant laughed quietly and came up behind her, tall and infinitely disturbing. His hands closed over the fine bones of her shoulders and he turned her towards him. "You're always telling me you hate me, little one. What can I do to change it?"

The moon was behind him and he looked dangerously intent and quite suddenly a stranger. Adrienne panicked. On a burst of pure instinct she slipped from under his hands and ran back through the thick springy grass . . . frog or no frogs.

The next morning Mrs. Manning was jubilant. The hours and hours of preparation forgotten, her mind was on the next money-making venture. Adrienne sat amazed. "Just think, dear – two thousand dollars clear, and that includes a donation!"

Adrienne didn't need two guesses as to the source of the donation. Mrs. Pink-Haired-Richest-Woman-in-Australia. Not only had she brought her pink hair to the party, but a pink beflowered evening hat to match. It had added considerably to the evening. Adrienne was just about to make some comment on it, when she was mercifully saved by a stroke of Providence. The owner of the hat and the hair, true to her colour scheme, came flowing through the glass doors in a pink chiffon and lace negligée. It would have graced any bride, but unfortunately did nothing for its wearer. Vera had followed in her wake. Both ladies had stayed over for the night, unknown to Adrienne. She had retired at one o'clock. The barbecue was still going strong then.

The voice when it came did not match the pink lady's appearance. It was a professional voice . . . a melodious contralto, controlled and cultured. "Good morning, young woman." Seen at close quarters, the faded eyes were shrewd and assessing . . . razor sharp, in fact. "At last we meet!"

Adrienne had sprung to her feet instinctively and was waved down for her trouble. The millionairess sank into a chair and Adrienne watched in fascination. She produced a long cigarette holder and made a business of lighting up . . . inhaling shallowly and exhaling gustily. Then she returned her attention to Adrienne. "Explain yourself, child." She stabbed the air briefly. "I kept asking who's the beauty, but no one had the decency to answer me."

"Oh, Lyla," Mrs. Manning spluttered into a fervent denial, "that's simply not true! I distinctly said that's Grant's secretary and my right-hand girl."

Lyla fenced her off with the holder. This proved to be an eye-stopping spectacle, for both old hands were adorned with what appeared to be an Australian gemstone collection. "Name yourself, child," she repeated.

Adrienne was very slightly nonplussed, but she tried to comply. "Name, Adrienne Brent. Age, twenty-two. Character, sometimes charming. Capacity, secretary to the household. Reason – one of them – to be away from Sydney." Nothing less than the truth would do.

Lyla threw up a gorgeous hand. "I knew it, I knew it!" she chortled. "There's a story in everything. You're Brent Engineering's girl. Married Madeleine Hamilton . . . quite a beauty . . . died about ten years ago . . . tragic. Married his secretary . . . cold-faced bitch." She punctuated the case-history graphically.

"Not his secretary," Adrienne amended. The old terror had everything else straight.

"No matter." Lyla lapsed into remembrance of things past. "It's coming back. That face . . . I knew I'd seen it before. Celine Hamilton, that's it! And what a snob she was too. Always looked like she'd been let loose among the savages." The old face fell into a million laugh-lines.

Adrienne couldn't deny it. It was quite true. Her grandmother's face had often worn just that expression. She met the old lady's eyes with amused comprehension.

"You're not one, I take it." Lyla looked closely at the

112

girl and liked what she saw. There was a strong look of her grandmother, but this girl had vivacity and sparkle Celine Hamilton had never chosen to display, at least not in public.

Vera looked on with loathing. So the insidious Adrienne was ingratiating herself with old Lyla, was she? Mrs. Manning had fallen for it as well. Vera had put herself out on many occasions for both of them with a noticeable lack of results. This Brent girl had the know-how she lacked. Vera did nothing without a motive. Adrienne's charm of manner must have a motivating factor. It just couldn't be natural, or so Vera imagined.

Grant walked into the room and the terrible old thing sailed into him. "I always said you were a dark horse, Grant."

One black eyebrow shot up. "You watch your tongue now, Lyla, or I'll have a pony saddled up for you!"

There was a vein of seriousness behind the banter. The mischievous old eyes came back to Adrienne and Adrienne felt herself shrinking from whatever was coming.

Grant walked over and took one of the loaded old hands. "Do you hear me, you notoriously wicked woman?"

"You won't charm me, lover," she chuckled, but managed to look it all the same. "Can't say I blame you," she muttered none too cryptically, and unexpectedly kissed him on the cheek. He bore it manfully.

Grant turned to the two girls. "Chris is coming over this afternoon. I thought we might take the horses out if you'd care to. We'll leave the sharpies here to their cards." Lyla, who was a card fanatic, had arranged a small bridge party for the afternoon.

Adrienne wasn't too sure. Chris was the easiest of companions, but an afternoon's riding with Grant would be something else again. For one thing he would make her nervous and all three of them, Vera, Chris and Grant were accomplished riders. She would be the only novice among them.

She said so to Grant later. "You might find me a bit of a nuisance."

The grey eyes glinted down at her. "Chris didn't appear to. I think we'll manage, Miss Faint Heart."

Adrienne's chin came up. "And what does that mean, for heaven's sake?"

"Well, aren't you?" He evaded the question tantalisingly.

She remained for a moment looking up at him, the light eyes so very aware of her, then she swung away from him uncertainly. "You're a born tease, Grant. Well, don't say I didn't warn you. If you say one nasty thing about my riding, I'll dismount and find my own way home. If I can—" she added thoughtfully. He laughed and went out of the house.

After lunch, at which Lyla mesmerised them with snippets of the stock market reports, they went down to the stables. Chris had been there first and saddled up the horses. Adrienne addressed the bent fair head. "Goldsborough Moreton are up two points. Castle Ridge is selling at a dollar fifty."

Chris looked up in startled surprise, then it dawned on him. "Old Lyla stay over, did she? You want to listen to her. They say she's worth a cool four million at the very least." He held the stirrup and she vaulted into the saddle. Chris started to laugh.

"No jokes, Chris. I'm on my mettle."

Grant and Vera rode ahead, and the others fell in behind them. This afternoon Vera was showing not the slightest sign of her late night. She was in her element. Adrienne was the merest novice in the saddle. One glance had told her that. She turned to Grant with her most charming smile, the one kept for him alone. "I think those two might make a match of it." She gave a light laugh. "Though I think Miss Brent might prove a bit of a handicap as a station wife!"

Grant slanted a look over his shoulder at the laughing

114

Adrienne. "She's beautiful enough to make you forget it, even if she has. I doubt it, though. She's remarkably efficient."

Vera gritted her teeth in impotent chagrin. She would have given a great deal to have disposed of Miss Adrienne Brent with one thrust, like the Borgias. That wasn't the answer she wanted. What had happened to Grant? She hadn't missed the interest behind the indulgence.

Somehow she found a smile. "Well, that's all to the good. It's about time Chris settled down. He's far too frivolous."

Grant turned in the saddle. "You can't be talking about Chris, Vera. He's a very hard-working young man. Marion has every reason to be proud of him."

Vera could have screamed with vexation. She and Grant seldom differed. She made sure of that. Hastily she turned the conversation into safer channels . . . the Saranga bloodstock. They fell into harmony.

At the back of them, Adrienne and Chris were laughing, or at least Chris was talking as usual and Adrienne was laughing. Their two horses jogged along contentedly and she let her hat slip off the back of her head. The sun was strong, but there was the faintest zephyr of a breeze and it stirred the dark hair at her temples.

At the foot of the rise Grant reined in. "Put that hat back on, Adrienne, or you'll have a headache by nightfall."

He was back to dictating, was he? Adrienne considered. She looked down at the strong brown hand holding the rein and seemed on the point of refusing, then she crammed it down over her ears.

"Very funny," he drawled, but his eyes were amused. He leaned over and righted the wide-brimmed cream hat, giving it a rakish tilt. He smiled suddenly and turned to Chris. "Doesn't look the part, does she?" Despite himself, Chris had to agree.

Adrienne looked from one to the other and appeared

115

put out. "The more I try, the less convincing I become." She slid to the ground. "I think I'll walk." Here was the opportunity she couldn't let pass. She sank down on a grassy patch and bent her head on to her knees. Her hair cascaded to one side and hid her face from them. She kept her head down.

Chris's voice shot up in concern. "Adrienne!" She looked the picture of dejection. Didn't she know Grant was only having a bit of fun?

Grant, however, was unperturbed. He swung to the ground and walked casually across to her. "Get up, Adrienne, we're not convinced." He pulled her to her feet in one movement and the dark eyes sparkled with suppressed merriment.

"Fooled you at least, Chris," she laughed up at him.

"You did too, you devious piece. I thought we'd mortally offended you. How fiendishly clever!"

Vera didn't think so. Her voice was absolutely colourless. "If we're quite finished with this boring little charade we might move on."

Adrienne couldn't control her quick flush and Grant swung her up into the saddle. His hand stayed at her waist. "Enough of your prankishness, Miss Brent. This Sunday riding is no fun."

Could it be possible he was being sarcastic at Vera's expense – Adrienne stole a look at the lean profile. It was quite bland, expressionless in fact.

The party moved on and Vera waited her opportunity. She had never been thwarted, not once in her twenty-seven years. Her father had made his money, and there was plenty of it, the hard way. He and his father before him had pioneered the wide open spaces, working with their bare hands. He didn't want his children to have to do the same. It had been a mistake. Vera and Brian had never known any form of opposition, parental or otherwise, and they didn't know how to handle it when it came. Harry Sterling was a fine man, but he had failed in the job of character-building. His children were not altogether to blame.

Adrienne could feel the green eyes boring into her. Surely it was unhealthy for Vera to be so obsessed with her rights of possession? She must be in her late twenties and Grant had known her from childhood. There had been plenty of time for him to make a move if one was forthcoming. Adrienne knew instinctively that she herself had not influenced that decision in any way. How she knew, despite Vera's broad hints and Mrs. Manning's warnings, she didn't quite know. She put it down to feminine intuition . . . a powerful force in female reckoning.

They bypassed the glade and came down on the willow-edged creek by another route. It was a winding track and quite steep in places. Grant led the way and Vera brought up the rear. Adrienne remembered thinking she would have preferred to have had Vera in front of her when three things happened simultaneously.

Vera gave Gemma a vicious prod from behind with the butt of her crop: Grant look over his shoulder to see how the others were progressing and saw Gemma plunge momentarily, unseating her inexperienced rider.

Chris's voice rang out through the bush, scattering the birds, "Adrienne!"

Grant was already off his horse and leaping down to the foot of the creek where Adrienne had fallen. She lay quite still. He ran his hands lightly over her – no bones broken; she was lucky. The ground was thickly padded. She had hit that boulder though. He parted the soft hair and found the bump easily. The skin was broken and there was a nasty swelling. It was bad enough to knock her out.

He cradled her head in his hands and looked up at the white-faced Vera. His own face was dark and frightening. It was all too much for Vera, who was aghast at the enormity of her own intentions. She was lucky at that – the girl was only stunned.

She wheeled her horse's head around. "I know when

I'm not wanted. I'll be off Saranga in an hour," she managed bitterly, and made up the track. At the top she broke into a gallop. That was it, finito. What she had read in Grant's eyes was absolutely final. Not that he had ever said anything. She had just taken it for granted that one day they would marry. She dug her heels in.

Down at the creek Adrienne had come to. A little colour crept back into her face and she looked up at the two faces so close to her. "What happened?" she croaked. It was hard to find her voice. To their surprise, she laughed, then wished she hadn't. Her head! Grant and Chris were unusually subdued, and Adrienne tried again. "Does everyone say 'what happened?' after a faint? I've never until this moment believed it."

Chris reached out and patted her cheek, and she turned her face into Grant's shirt. She had remembered what happened, but where was Vera? No one told her.

Grant made a brisk return to his usual manner. "Well, you're the world's worst horsewoman, so I'll take you up with me." He looked across at Chris. "Get Evans out, like a good lad. I don't think there's anything much wrong with her, but I'd like to be sure."

Chris sprang to his feet and leapt into the saddle. "Right-oh! Be a good girl," he called somewhat unnecessarily to Adrienne. She was prostrate.

Adrienne lay back. "Not much wrong with her!" Ye gods, her head was throbbing and Grant's face seemed blurry. She reached up to touch it. "Your face is going out of focus, Grant."

He caught her hand and held it. "Tell me when it isn't."

She closed her eyes again and waited for the world to stop rocking. After a while she looked up and found the grey eyes steady. Unconsciously his thumb was caressing her cheekbone and Adrienne spoke gently. "It's all right, Grant. Everything has righted itself." His eyes had darkened or the pupils had enlarged because he looked quite different . . . grave and introspective. She sighed deeply. "I could stay here for ever."

The firm mouth curved. The spell was broken. "I would say it was a fairly compromising position, my girl." He laughed softly to himself and then lifted her with infinite gentleness into his arms, rising to his feet. "I'll take you up with me. Just relax and we'll be home in no time." He put her up on to the horse and mounted behind her, settling her comfortably back in his arms. His mouth came down close to her ear. "Relax, honey, for heaven's sake. Close your eyes."

She did what she was told. She had spoken the truth back there, she could stay close to him for ever. But her head was aching too much for her to worry whether he knew it or not. Grant's arm tightened around her and he turned his mount's head for home.

When Vera arrived at the homestead her chastened mood had given way to pure rage and thwarted desire. The bridge party looked up startled. Anyone with half an eye could see that something catastrophic had happened.

Mrs. Manning viewed the taut face with alarm. "Why, Vera, whatever has happened? Where are the others?"

Vera was past pandering to Mrs. Manning. She swung through the glass doors with one savage movement, totally ignoring the other women and not even glancing in Mrs. Manning's direction.

"The bitch has been thwarted, I'd say." Lyla went into a paroxysm of coughing. Her doctor had given her six months thirty years ago. Mrs. Manning gazed back at her uncomprehendingly, and Lyla recovered herself. "Play cards, play cards!" she barked. No talk of Vera was going to spoil her hand. Mrs. Manning returned to the game. No one argued with Lyla.

When Chris came bounding up the front stairs ten minutes later that was the end of it. Lyla was disgusted. She hadn't had time to recoup her losses. "We might as well wind it up, girls." She slammed her cards down on the table. Mrs. Manning had long since lost interest in the game. Through the open window they saw Vera's Mercedes run down the drive. She had her foot down too.

"Tell us, son, before it proves fatal." Lyla sat back and lit up. She was beginning to enjoy herself.

Chris turned to Mrs. Manning. "Adrienne's had a fall." Mrs. Manning's face blanched and he hurried on. "Don't worry, she's all right, but Grant wants Doc Evans out as a precaution." Helen was through to the phone in an instant.

"Push her, did she?" Lyla stated, not questioned. It was as well the other ladies had tactfully dispersed.

"Don't go putting words into my mouth, you scandalous old woman!" Chris went up to her and shook her hand. Everyone knew Lyla Duncan. Not many people, however, were brave enough to call her a scandalous old woman. In her younger days she had been a dangerous woman as well. She still had her days.

"You can't fool me, boy. I've been around too long. Harry Sterling has ruined his two. I told him years ago, but he wouldn't listen. No one listens," she added gleefully.

"Well, I for one will," Chris replied. He was intent on diverting her attention. "Come over here and give me a run down on the stock market."

Once Lyla got her teeth into anything she wouldn't let go – a canine characteristic, not at all at variance with her appearance. For once Lyla was sidetracked. The one thing she placed above the latest gossip was the latest fluctuations. She talked and Chris listened. After a while he shifted over from one ear to the two. By the sound of it, it would cost him money if he didn't.

When Grant and Adrienne arrived back, Dr. Evans was talking to Mrs. Manning on the veranda where she had come out to greet him. They turned and watched the two come up to them. Adrienne appeared to be all right. She was walking well, though Grant had an arm around her.

Mrs. Manning took her straight through to her room and the doctor followed.

Lyla decided to tackle Grant. "Been up to it, has she, the murderous bitch?" Her old face was twitching with the scent of a good story.

Grant walked over to the cabinet and poured himself a stiff drink. "Leave it alone, Lyla, or I'll have to put it around how you took down the Fielding Trading Company."

The little face worked. "You wouldn't, you know. No one would believe you."

Grant burst out laughing and she was forced to join in. Of course they would. Everyone would believe him, and why not? It was perfectly true. Not that she had any qualms about it. She would do it again. Grant mixed her a gin and tonic and went out of the room.

Chris had strolled through to the veranda to await the doctor's verdict. Doctor Evans wasn't unduly perturbed. There was slight concussion. He had dressed the swelling, not to his satisfaction. Adrienne had flatly refused to allow him to cut away some of her hair, and Mrs. Manning had upheld the decision, so he administered a sedative and left her to rest. Chris waited until the all clear was given and then walked the doctor to his car. He couldn't get home quick enough himself. Just wait until he told Mum! He waved a hand to Grant who had come out with them and pulled away. Grant watched him out of sight, then went through to Adrienne's rooms.

It was after six and Helen had left on the bedside lamp. The shade was an antique gold to match the quilted satin bedspread and it threw a warm glow over the pale face on the pillow. Adrienne sat up a little in the bed. Thank goodness, she thought, that her nightdress was adequate. It had a high round neck and row upon row of smocking. She pushed back her tumbled hair, drowsy with the effects of the drug.

Grant stood at the foot of the bed, then leant over,

smiling a little. "You look very fragile sitting up there and much more at home than you do on a horse."

Adrienne watched, startled, while he came round the side of the bed. Her eyes went huge. His masculinity was overwhelming in the small room.

"Oh, Adrienne," he mocked her softly, "how your eyes do give you away! Did you think I was going to kiss you?" She smiled ruefully. She was nearly asleep.

He moved suddenly. The dark head came down and blocked out the light. His lips brushed her cheek, then moved across to her mouth. He held her face up to him and kissed her slowly and thoroughly. It was a very adult kiss and Adrienne felt faint with unaccustomed emotion. She held on to the lapel of his shirt. He took his time then lifted his head. His skin was copper in the lamplight, the grey eyes twin points of light. Adrienne clung to him as all that was steady in the whirling room.

"I couldn't disappoint you, now, could I?"

He held her chin, but at the laugh in his voice she swung away from him and turned face down in the pillows. She felt his hand on her hair, then he was gone, clicking the door softly behind him. Adrienne lay where she was, her heart hammering. She had been kissed before, but never like that. She could still feel his mouth moving against hers. She groaned aloud, then drifted quickly into oblivion.

CHAPTER SEVEN

THE next day Lyla left and the piano arrived, but Adrienne wasn't allowed up to see either event. When Mrs. Ford came in with the morning tray, she asked Adrienne what she would like for lunch and by the sounds of it was prepared to go to some lengths to get it. Vera had flung through the kitchen yesterday and little by little Mrs. Ford had pieced the story together. She didn't say much, but she missed very little of what went on in the household. She stooped over and plumped up the pillows behind the girl's back, waiting for her answer.

Adrienne smiled and picked up her fruit juice – it was deliciously cold. "Don't worry, Mrs. Ford, I'll be up long before then."

Mrs. Ford wisely said nothing. Grant had told her about Adrienne's accident and asked him to prepare the trays. He obviously intended her to stay where she was all day and he had always had his way for as long as Mrs. Ford could remember. This young lady was in for an awakening. She watched her finish her grapefruit juice, then turned to the door, murmuring, "Well, we'll see what we shall see."

When Mrs. Ford had gone she started on her scrambled eggs with fingers of hot buttered toast. Whatever Mrs. Ford did to plain scrambled eggs she resolved to find out. She took a sip of her coffee. This was marvellous, she thought – well worth getting a crack on the head for. Though it was no joke she had it in her heart to feel sorry for Vera. One couldn't blame her for loving Grant, she was bowled over herself. But why hadn't she thought of it before? Grant must have encouraged her. She frowned. Of course he had. Grant had encouraged her. How else could Vera have become so involved? She put down the cup.

123

How easy it was to fool oneself. She knew there was an attraction between Grant and herself. Attraction! What an inadequate word to describe her feelings for him. Didn't she love him, or at least was madly in love with him? She wasn't naïve enough to think it was the same thing. He was – what? – twelve years older than she and very experienced, judging by his kiss. She had been kissed before and it had been nothing like that. What was it he wanted? If anything? She frowned again, remembering Vera. He could be a rich philanderer – but, to be fair, an exceedingly hard-working rich philanderer, if there was such a thing. His energy left her breathless, let alone his kisses.

Adrienne picked up her coffee, a little comforted, then put it down again with a resounding rattle. Ugh, it was cold! The time she spent debating with herself about Grant. He should be flattered . . . the rich roué. That was it! Rich roué. Her mood had swung with a vengeance. She got up, had a quick shower and dressed. Her head had started up again. She wasn't as well as she thought she was. She was just brushing her hair when there was a tap on the door. She braced herself and called, "Come in!" It was probably Mrs. Manning and she was anxious to look well enough to start the day.

Adrienne looked into the mirror, startled. Grant was walking towards her. He wasted no time on preliminaries. "What do you think you're doing?"

There was no stopping Adrienne. "I should say it was fairly obvious, Grant. I'm brushing my hair. I intend to do some work this morning." He raised an eyebrow, smiling at the crispness of her tone. She knew he was laughing at her and her voice was very cool indeed. "I hope you're not going to object. After all, that's what I'm here for."

His look was interested. "What brought this on, Adrienne? Your defence mechanism working, I take it."

There was an unmistakable dash of humour in his voice and Adrienne found her indignation evaporating like so much perfume in the air. But it left its effect. "Oh, go

124

away, Grant!" She bit her lip and seemed on the point of crying.

"Now don't go complicated on me, child. Take off that dress and get back into bed."

She looked down, her eyes brimming with tears. Wouldn't you think he would just go!

"Adrienne—" He pulled her into his arms, his voice a caress. "Leave things as they are, little one. You've had a bad knock and I want you to rest. Is that so terrible?" The words went on deep and lulling and she was unable to argue with him. The tension went out of her and she turned back to the bed. Grant watched her in silence, then strode to the door. "By the way, the piano has arrived. You can try it out tomorrow. I'll have someone take a look at it this afternoon."

She had to detain him. "But Grant, who's to open the mail?"

The light eyes were teasing. "Do you think I can't manage without you, Miss Brent? Pretty soon now I won't be able to manage with you."

"Oh, Grant," she murmured, and pulled at the bed-spread abstractedly. He seemed about to speak, then changed his mind and went out with a careless wave of his hand.

Adrienne's head was well and truly thumping, so she undressed and got back into bed. She had a very quiet day, listening to the tuner picking at random notes and then breaking into a grand slam of his own particular party piece. Why was it that tuners couldn't play very well?

When Mrs. Manning came in, she at least made something of the day by confessing in all earnestness that they had nourished a viper in their bosoms. Adrienne had thought the expression extinct.

The next morning Adrienne was in the office early to collect the mail. Yesterday's had been sorted. Grant must have found time to do it. She felt much better and had been most emphatic when Mrs. Manning had enquired after her health at breakfast. Her first time off a horse wasn't going to turn her into an invalid.

She riffled through the mail and sorted it quickly. She was anxious to get down to work, though being at Saranga was more like helping out in a well-loved home than doing an organised job. When had this feeling of utter belonging started? Perhaps from her first glimpse of the jacarandas. They had seemed like an omen to her; a benign and beautiful omen. Saranga. she realised with a small sense of shock, was far more of a home to her than the beautiful new house her father had built for his second wife. Of course, Linda had refused point blank to live in the home Adrienne had grown up in. Adrienne frowned and came back to business. She switched on the typewriter and listened to its businesslike hum. Even the most sophisticated woman got a kick out of some manual work well done. Adrienne worked steadily through the day and didn't see Grant until dinnertime.

He looked down the table at her. "Do we have the pleasure of hearing you this evening, Miss Lympany?"

"Pleasure's the word," Mrs. Manning broke in. "I know you told me not to listen, Adrienne, but it was very difficult not to, even with the lid down."

Adrienne had found time for an hour's practice in the late afternoon. She hadn't touched a piano for six weeks, and that was an age to a musician. She thought of the time she had had to play at functions and the sick hollow feeling in the pit of her stomach, but this was different. She knew she would enjoy it.

After dinner, they moved into the living room and Grant opened up the piano for her. It was a beautiful instrument, a six-foot Bechstein concert grand in gleaming ebony. Adrienne felt a ripple of excitement and the peculiar anticipatory sensation of feeling the smooth keys under her fingers before she even approached the piano.

Mrs. Manning was settling back in her chair for all the

world as if she was attending a concert with the rare privilege of being able to bring her own seating. Grant said nothing, but moved back and found his usual armchair.

Adrienne crossed to the piano, sat down and ran her fingers over the keys, feeling the weight of them. Every piano was different, and one had to know how they would react. It was much the same as running through the gears on a strange car. She frowned a little in concentration, then broke into Debussy's *La Plus que Lente*. It was a haunting, rather morbidly nostalgic little piece and it gave her time to settle her nerves and judge the dynamics of the piano.

Neither Grant nor Mrs. Manning spoke when she finished, so she kept on playing – Ravel, Schumann, Rachmaninoff and inevitably Chopin. She had forgotten her audience now and felt the full power flow into her fingers. She stopped abruptly in the middle of a waltz and started into the *Ocean Etude*. It came as she wanted it.

It was fully a minute before anyone spoke, then Mrs. Manning lifted her head from the wing of the chair. "Thank you, my dear, that was pure enchantment."

Involuntarily Adrienne's eyes sought Grant's. He smiled into the dark eyes. "You play beautifully, child. We're very impressed."

Adrienne got up and closed down the lid of the piano. She had been playing just on an hour, and she had enjoyed it far more than her audience. That was the performer's special compensation for the hours and hours of hard work behind the scenes. She felt perfectly at peace, all tension was released. . . . From then on, the piano was played daily. Indeed it was expected by the household. Grant had even suggested an hour's practice in the morning. As far as he was concerned, Adrienne could arrange her own time-table. The work was being attended to, and very capably, and that was all he cared about.

Adrienne thought it was very generous of him and told him so at morning dictation. His eyes glimmered with amusement. "I take it, then, you're getting over your initial disappointment, Miss Brent."

Adrienne put down her pencil and rested her chin in her hand. "What a beast you were to me that day! I can't remember ever having disliked someone so much on sight," she remarked quite untruthfully.

"I did ask Horton to send me a competent woman secretary," he said. "One I fondly imagined with a good capable face and round glasses, but instead he sent me a dark-eyed, camelia-skinned, outspoken little creature, ready to take me to task and the interview out of my hands."

Adrienne stared back at him. How like a man to be so unreasonable!

"A significant silence, Miss Brent. Why don't you admit it?"

She was quite frank with him. "You can't be serious, Grant. Anyone would have reacted the way I did. You were so terribly starchy and overbearing."

He laughed and reached for a cigarette. "Not anyone, Adrienne. Just you." He lit the cigarette without taking his eyes off her, looking so overwhelmingly male and vital that it was all Adrienne could do to stay in her chair. "You know, you're hardly tame, little one."

Adrienne gazed at him in astonishment. He seemed to be serious, but he couldn't be! "I don't understand you, Grant, but thank you for allowing me time to practise, I do appreciate it."

"What nice manners, Miss Brent," he murmured, and handed over a sheaf of typescript. "You'll notice a few amendments. I'm sorry I had to spoil your typing. It was unavoidable, I'm afraid." He crushed out his half-smoked cigarette. "I'd better be off. I've some business in Cooyong." He moved off the table where he had been sitting and went out the door with a brief salute.

Adrienne looked down the pages. A few amendments! Why, he'd ruined the lot. She had made such a nice job of it too. Ah well, hers was not to reason why. She put paper in the machine. This would take time.

When Grant returned in the afternoon he found Adrienne in a rare state of agitation. She was poised in the middle of the room, her whole bearing tense. She pounced on him the minute he came in. "Thank goodness you're back, Grant. There's a mouse in the office. It's been running round all afternoon. If you don't catch it, I'll go out of my mind."

He looked at her quickly. She often spoke extravagantly, but this time he could see she was genuinely het up. He kept his voice level. "The cheek of it! I suppose it's come in from the garden. I expect it wanted company."

"Oh, Grant!" She was really quite jumpy. "It's run from one side to the other and just ignored me. I threw that folder at it and missed." She pointed to a heavy spring-backed folder still lying on the floor. "I'm nearly mad."

Grant tried, but couldn't make it. He laughed. At that precise moment the minute offender scurried from behind the cabinet and shot through the door as though all the bats of hell were after him. Adrienne moved hastily alongside Grant and he patted her shoulder comfortingly, much as he would one of his spirited fillies. "Don't worry, Adrienne. I'll get a sign up, No Visitors. That should take care of it." She shuddered violently – she couldn't help it. "Frogs, mice, horses, strange men in your room! What a nervy little thing you are, to be sure." He gave her a shake. "Well, were you able to finish that script for me?"

Adrienne came back to business with a jolt. "Of course," she answered irritably, then collected herself. "Of course, Mr. Manning," she amended carefully.

The grey eyes snapped. "That's much better, Adrienne. I can see I'll have to give you a slapping down occasionally just to keep you in hand."

Adrienne felt a little apprehensive. She was inclined to go too far. She passed him the typescript and he took it, scanned it briefly and went out of the room. A few moments later she heard the Mercedes purr to life and she felt guilty for having detained him with such frivolous things as mice. Adrienne sighed and hoped it wouldn't come back all the same. It was too hot to close the door.

At dinner that evening, Grant made quite a story of the afternoon's smallest incident. If he was hoping to strike an answering chord of derision in Mrs. Manning, he was doomed to disappointment. That lady controlled a fastidious shudder. "How despicable! We must have it attended to."

Grant was much amused. "You're welcome to, Helen, if you can catch it."

Adrienne looked him straight in the eye. "You know, Grant, if you're really looking for someone to enjoy the joke, you'd better wait until you see Chris."

Grant laughed and let the matter drop. For the time being anyway.

Chris did hear the story when he came over on the Friday to see some of the Moreton stock running. Grant looked in after lunch and asked Adrienne if she would care to come down and see a trial run.

She didn't hesitate. "Oh yes, please, Grant." She got to her feet eagerly and Grant ran his eyes over her slim linen skirt.

"You'd better change into slacks. You might want to sit on the fence." For the life of her, Adrienne couldn't control a blush. "Not that I don't admire a good pair of legs, Adrienne, but we'll be wanting to watch the horses."

Adrienne was slightly exasperated with him and showed it. She stalked past him without speaking and he called after her, "Don't be long, I haven't got all day." He still sounded amused. Her long slim legs vanished round the door. She was back in under five minutes. The grey glance slipped over the blue and white striped cotton knit and the

130

matching blue slacks, and this time she was definitely annoyed.

"You notice things far too much, Grant," she said crossly.

The light eyes were deliberately quizzical. "By things do you mean you, Adrienne?"

She wasn't going to fence with him. She walked out the door into the sunshine. Grant came up behind her and took her arm, pacing her along to the training ground. He was in quite a good humour, it seemed.

It was the first time Adrienne had ever been there and she looked round her with interest. The sun was high, the grass was green and the fence was white. The horses and riders were already out on the track. There were four of them. On and around the fence were perhaps twenty hands, all of them smoking, and all of them without exception had their eyes glued on the opposite side of the track. Adrienne couldn't see Grant's concern. Not one of them had so much as glanced in her direction. Racquel Welch could have made a complete circuit of the track without turning a head, she thought – the first time round anyway.

Grant swung her easily on to the fence and she twined her legs in the lower rungs. She didn't feel any too safe. She watched him take out his stop watch and nod to his leading hand. The starting pistol went off and they were away.

Even to Adrienne it was exciting. All four jockeys rode in the Australian style with short stirrups and curved backs. The men had suddenly found their voices and called all sorts of encouragement liberally peppered with the great Australian adjective.

The first time round the horses seemed evenly matched, but on the second circuit, the biggest, a beautiful bay, stretched out and covered the ground like a champion finishing a good length and a half in front. Grant pressed down his stopwatch the minute it flashed past the post. He too seemed excited, although he hadn't reached the swear-

131

ing stage. Adrienne watched him vault the fence and make over to the riders who were patting their mounts and rubbing them down with a great deal of affection.

Adrienne had a different picture of Grant. This was his life, after all. He was a man of the great outdoors. It made his eyes light up and take fences at a leap. It was a life she wasn't used to. She had loved watching the horses. They were magnificent animals, but these people out here were quite different. She looked round. There they were banging one another on the back and throwing their hats down and jumping on them and generally behaving in a thoroughly uncivilised fashion. She laughed aloud and one of the hands turned in surprise.

He tipped his understandably battered old hat and came up to her. "Did you see that, miss? That young Robbie can whisper them in, the b . . . the little beauty!"

Adrienne smiled at him. It was a bit late in the day for minding his language. "Then Robbie's your Scobie. I thought it was the horse that won it."

Her well-weathered informant spat fastidiously. "Oh, the horse! The horse is a champion all right. Should be, by Regal Ruler out of Tudor Gold."

Adrienne felt like saying it looks like it's out by the fence, but thought better of it. They were all so serious. Evidently the time had been impressive. She had been too long in the city.

Adrienne watched Chris slide off his mount and he looked up and waved. She waved back and nearly came off the fence. Her new-found friend came to her aid with alacrity. "Steady there, miss. You nearly came a cropper."

Grant was across in a few strides, torn between amusement and concern. "Good grief, Adrienne, you're a danger to yourself." He swung her off the fence and kept a steadying hand on her. She landed lightly and surprised a rather curious expression on Chris's face. He looked as if he had found his idol had a seat of clay.

132

She read him correctly. "Were you wondering if I was accident-prone, Chris?" She laughed up at him. His expression relaxed. Adrienne didn't feel in the least bit ashamed of her lack of a good seat on a fence or a horse. It simply wasn't important to her. She turned to Grant. "What relation to Mountain Gold is Tudor Gold?"

Chris laughed and even Grant took time answering her. "Actually, Adrienne, they're in no way related, but it was an inspired guess."

She looked from one to the other. "Oh, I don't mind your laughing in the least. I imagine there are lots of things I know that you two don't."

Grant's hand slid down the length of her shiny hair. "Such as?"

"The first three place-getters in the Melbourne Cup since its inception."

Chris was visibly impressed, but Grant merely gave a small tug to an end curl. "Well, we won't embarrass you by asking."

Actually she couldn't name last year's favourite, let alone the winner. Adrienne thought it was time she made herself scarce. "Thank you for letting me come down, Grant. I really enjoyed it, even if I don't know much about it."

Chris didn't think that state of affairs unalterable. "You could easily learn, Adrienne, if you wanted to." He brushed himself down. "I'll come back to the house with you. I have a message for Helen."

Adrienne caught Grant's eyes and a flash of mockery came into them. "Any excuse is better than none, I suppose. All right then, Chris, don't be long, we're not finished here yet." He watched them go, then turned back to the men, who seemed to be counting their wages or something like that.

Chris ran an appreciative eye over the girl at his side. "Adrienne, my love, you seem to be getting better-looking every time I see you, and that's saying something."

Adrienne laughed. "Don't run along, Chris. I won't be able to get a hat on soon." The dark eyes she turned up to him were soft and sweetly feminine. Chris groaned aloud and kept up the banter all the way to the house. Adrienne had her work cut out parrying his compliments. They looked very young and carefree together. Mrs. Manning watched them from the house. What a pity they didn't match! She was very fond of Chris; as straightforward and uncomplicated a young man as you could wish for. Adrienne on the other hand was a rather highly-strung girl of many facets. It just wouldn't do. They only had their youth and high spirits in common, and it just wasn't enough. Chris might try, but he would never appreciate her musicianship, for instance. You only had to look at Adrienne's face as she played to realise how important it was to her. Chris really needed someone like that young Donaldson girl – a pretty, capable girl, and equally uncomplicated. What a pity Chris didn't think so. He was smitten with Adrienne, it was plain to see. It was equally apparent to Mrs. Manning that Adrienne was strongly attracted to Grant, but he persisted in treating her like a precocious child. Such a lovely girl too, and so gifted! Ah well, they would have to work it out for themselves. She sighed and turned away from the window.

Chris stopped in the hallway to admire the lilies. Mrs. Manning had liked them so much in that position that there they remained. He fingered a petal gently. "Do you know, I've seen these dozens of times and never really noticed them until now."

Mrs. Manning came through to them with a quotation. "Solomon in all his glory was not arrayed as one of these."

Chris straightened up and kissed her. "Just got up from your Bible, Helen?"

"You know I never miss a quotation, Chris. Seriously though, I don't think Solomon could have had much in the way of clothes." Chris looked at her thoughtfully. He had often suspected her of wandering. Mrs. Manning might have sensed his thoughts, for she elaborated kindly, "I've been through the Middle East, as you know, and the lilies of the field—! They're very humble indeed. Nothing like these glorious specimens, I assure you."

Chris was convinced. "Well, you can't take much notice of the Bible," he clinched it irreverently. "By the way, I have a note from Mum. I'll spoil it by telling you Lyla is dead set on being the hostess with the mostest. Aunt Sara got wind of it in Sydney and let Mum know."

"Is she indeed?" Mrs. Manning was perusing the note. "So she is, the twerp." Adrienne and Chris laughed out loud. The word sounded incongruous on Mrs. Manning's ladylike lips. She looked at them, her eyes far away. "I have some ideas of my own." She pronounced it much in the way of a magician about to produce not one but two bunnies from the hat. But she didn't enlighten them further.

Chris turned to Adrienne with a grin. "This will cost us money, I know." He stayed on talking for a while, then went back to the training ground. Grant was waiting, and no one kept Grant waiting.

CHAPTER EIGHT

FOR the next few weeks, Adrienne saw hardly anything of Grant. He was out on the run from early morning until sundown and at dinner seemed very preoccupied. Adrienne tackled him one night over coffee. Mrs. Manning had one of her "heads" and had retired for the night.

She set her cup down carefully. "You seem terribly busy and distracted, Grant. What's happening?"

He turned to look at her and she felt her heart start to hammer in the most peculiar way. His look was almost a physical touch. She was fairly certain he was recalling having kissed her, and her eyes were as brilliant then as they were now. The hectic colour rushed to her cheeks. "What's happening, Adrienne?" he repeated in an easy teasing tone. "Well, this is a busy time of the year for the station, some of my stock are missing, nothing to worry about, but I mean to find out, and I have one or two other things on my mind." His mouth twitched. "It's very distracting."

"You sound like that's a silly word."

Grant smiled. "No one has ever told me I looked distracted before. I was savouring it."

Adrienne felt mildly exasperated as she always did when she was with him. "Why don't you take me seriously, Grant? You're always having a laugh at my expense."

The grey eyes glinted. "If I took you seriously, child, where would I be? Especially as I'm so busy."

Adrienne drew in her breath and leaned back against the cushions. Her face changed, and the look of wanting gave way to an aristocratic indifference. Grant lifted his head and seemed about to say something placating, then changed his mind. He smiled at the now familiar tilt of her head and said nothing. Adrienne stole a glance at him from under her lashes. She had felt sure he would say something. He really did seem a little tired and withdrawn.

She relented her pre-selected mood of aggrieved silence. "Could I ride out with the men sometimes, Grant? I could help with the sheep or the cattle."

Grant gave a shout of laughter, his tiredness completely dissipated. "Good grief, Adrienne, the things you say! Definitely not, child. You'd get trampled on first go and then where would I be?" His eyes were very bright.

Adrienne got to her feet with as much dignity as she could muster. Grant was still laughing and it made it that much more difficult. "I was only trying to be of help. Tammy Donaldson is able to do it, but I assume she was born in the saddle."

Grant put out a placating hand and against her better judgement Adrienne found her own in his. He stroked the palm of her hand with his thumb. The tricks of him! "You don't really want to ride around like one of the hands, do you, Adrienne? Tammy is needed on her father's property, but you don't have to do that here." His mouth compressed, but he went on. "It was very thoughtful of you to offer." Adrienne was silent and he shook her hand. "I was going to ask you to play for me. I could do with some soothing."

She looked at him with suspicion, but he appeared quite serious. "Very well, Grant." She went to the piano. "What would you like?"

"Nothing too stimulating. I feel like relaxing not being stirred."

Adrienne began to play a piece she didn't care for, though it was wonderfully evocative of it's name – *Clair de Lune*. She had played about twelve bars when Grant's voice broke into the moonlight and tall trees. "I can't say why exactly, but I don't like that piece."

Adrienne laughed briefly. "Neither do I, but it is restful."

She racked her brains trying to think of something to

follow. She rather specialised in making the keyboard sound. Her hands came down on the *Raindrop Prelude* and straight away Grant laughed. "Adrienne dear, play some Bach or Scarlatti, identifiable by number only." He lit a cigarette, closed his eyes and leant back. There was a smile on his face.

Adrienne ignored him and played as she felt like it. The Albeniz *Evocation* seemed appropriate. About half an hour later she turned on the piano seat. Good grief, Grant was asleep! Thank goodness he slept with his mouth shut. It would be awful if he didn't. She thought what did it have to do with her how Grant slept, then tiptoed across and leant over him. Immediately his eyes flew open.

He reached out for her and pulled her down to him. "Tell me what you were thinking."

Adrienne was truthful. "I was thinking what a good thing you sleep with your mouth shut." Then it occurred to her. "But then you weren't asleep, were you?"

It was too much for Grant. He swung to his feet, bringing her with him. "A good thing for whom?" He watched her colour mount, then laughed. "Do you know, Adrienne, I think you're quite mad." He turned her towards the door. "Look in on Helen on your way to bed."

"Am I being dismissed, Grant?" She looked at him over her shoulder.

"Yes, my dear, you are. You're one reason why I'm looking so distracted."

Adrienne made a tutting sound and didn't say goodnight to him. He didn't deserve it. She knocked gently on Mrs. Manning's door and waited until she was told to come in.

Mrs. Manning was sitting up in bed with a pile of pillows, all lace-edged, Adrienne noted, behind her. A pair of very functional-looking tortoiseshell glasses were perched on her nose. To the best of her knowledge, Adrienne had never seen sight nor sign of them or their case since she arrived. They looked convincing. "Come in, dear, come in. I could hear the piano." She lighted on Grant's very word – "So soothing."

Adrienne was having a great deal of trouble focusing her attention on the figure in the bed. At first glance, Mrs. Manning's bedroom appeared to be furnished with rare and beautiful antiques. Adrienne's quick eye, and it had to be, fell on a Queen Anne bureau and matching walnut card table, as well as four or five paintings of eighteenth-century vintage. She would count them later. There were also a gorgeous Bokhara rug and what looked like a Regency stool, all carved and gilded, converted to a marble-topped table on which stood a Meissen-type figure. It *was* Meissen. Adrienne tried desperately not to goggle. She had a curious sensation of having drifted back in a ripple of time to the eighteenth century. She sank down gingerly on one of the Louis XV chairs feeling like a lady in waiting.

Mrs. Manning had not missed any of it. "Do you like my things, Adrienne?" She gazed around fondly. The pillows had slipped down and revealed the carved gilt and damask headboard of her bed.

Adrienne smiled. "Things indeed, Mrs. Manning! The room is exquisite, so is the rest of the house for that matter."

"We're all collectors, dear. It runs in the family. Grant brought back the chandeliers and the Venetian mirror as well from London. He had the dickens' own job getting the pair." She sighed. "As for me, I've nothing else. No husband, no children. My treasures are my children, they console me."

I should think they would, Adrienne thought.

Mrs. Manning threw off her slight shade of depression. It was not altogether unpleasant, especially when you looked around at her "children". "I've been toying with the idea of having a picnic race day ball combined affair. What do you think of it?

Adrienne thought it staggeringly ambitious, but hesi-

139

tated to say so. "It sounds a marvellous idea, Mrs. Manning, but a tremendous amount of work, surely?"

Mrs. Manning pushed her glasses back on her nose. She really did need them. "Work, yes, but I've been thinking of taking the wind out of Lyla's sails. She mentioned to Marion that she had an interest in the new wing. Why, I'm sure I don't know. It's not as though she would be likely to use it," she commented irrelevantly and rather unfairly. "I want to get in before her. I don't think she could come up with anything better."

"I entirely agree, Mrs. Manning, but don't you think it would be too much for you all the same . . . all that work?" Adrienne was trying to head her off. She actually thought it would finish up being too much for her as well. Mrs. Manning was undoubtedly the Chief, but she required a great many little Indians.

Mrs. Manning was triumphant. "As to that, my dear, I'll use a little more organisation."

Adrienne managed a gesture of assent. She thought her voice would fail her. She rose smilingly. "I won't disturb you any longer, Mrs. Manning – naturally I'll help you in any way I can."

Mrs. Manning took off her glasses and placed them tenderly on the Queen Anne table which stood beside her bed. Adrienne wasn't sure if she was protecting the glasses or the table. The lady turned. "I know, dear, I know, and I'm counting on you."

Adrienne wilted a little, but managed to keep her end up. She smiled goodnight and overcame the temptation to back ceremoniously from the room. The furnishings and Mrs. Manning's regality had all but unnerved her. On her way to her room she noticed the light on in Grant's study which was separate from the office. Adrienne tapped on the door and Grant looked up. "I'll see you at the picnic race day ball," she whispered.

One eyebrow went up as far as it would go. "You'll what?"

Adrienne put a finger to her lips and crept silently away like a good little Indian. It was on, and the big wheels were rolling.

Grant almost put a spoke in them at breakfast. "I might as well finance the whole thing and be done with it. It will come off in taxes anyway." He looked vaguely thunderous. "I do think it's too much, Helen."

Mrs. Manning was distressed. "But, Grant dear, no one wants you to do that. It's a communal effort, don't you see?"

Grant saw all right. "Well, unless it's a communal effort as far as the work is concerned, it would be better dropped. I don't want to see you exhausted, and there's nothing much of Adrienne."

Mrs. Manning was unusually insistent. She could just see Lyla coming up with something downright spectacular. "I promise you, dear, things will be better organised. The ladies are really quite wonderful when it comes to it."

Grant downed his coffee very hot. He looked and felt excessively irritated. "See the ladies get asked," he remarked with heavy sarcasm, and strode from the room.

"What's up with the dear boy?" Mrs. Manning's voice was completely devoid of sarcasm. She was merely anxious.

Adrienne answered her. "Grant's going non-stop, Mrs. Manning, and working late at night. I expect he's tired."

"Oh, say no more, don't I know it!" Mrs. Manning looked upwards excessively, then promptly forgot it. It was obvious that she thought of Grant as a dynamo with enormous untapped reserves of energy. She quite over-looked the fact that Grant got tired the same as lesser mortals. After breakfast, Adrienne went through to the office and Mrs. Manning was already on the phone. By the end of the day the plans for the picnic race day ball were laid. "Yes, Agnes, it will be a money-spinner."

Adrienne smiled satirically. "Let's hope Agnes showed her face as well as her purse," she thought.

141

Grant wasn't in to dinner, which was unusual as he always left word whether he would be in or not. By ten o'clock Adrienne started to feel alarmed. She allowed her intuition to tell her something was wrong. Mrs. Manning didn't share her fears.

"I'm turning in, dear. I've had a big day." She had, at that.

Adrienne murmured absentmindedly, "Very sensible, Mrs. Manning. But where is Grant?"

The older woman looked down at her thoughfully. Things were getting rather involved. Here was Adrienne asking, "Where is Grant?" with her heart in her eyes. It was too bad. She essayed an answer. "Don't worry, my dear, almost anything could have kept him. Wherever he is he'll certainly know how to look after himself." She was not given to demonstrative gestures, but she patted the gleaming head as she passed. "Goodnight, my dear. Rest assured Grant is quite all right."

About half-past eleven, Adrienne heard the crunch of footsteps on the gravel of the drive. Instinctively she knew they were Grant's and she flew to the front door and out into the night. The sky was clear and bright with stars but the garden was a secret place where no moonlight touched.

"Is that you, Grant?" she called, her heart hammering with nervous relief. She flew towards him and he caught her up and swung her off her feet. "I thought it was the rustlers!" she gasped in a panic.

Grant laughed. "Do you do this deliberately or are you just plain crazy?"

Adrienne subsided thankfully against him. Grant was home and that was all that mattered. "Oh, Grant, you did tell me the stock was going off, and you always say whether you'll be home to dinner. I thought it must be rustlers."

His laughter fanned her cheek. "Thieves, Adrienne, thieves. Leave the rustlers to Burt Lancaster." He walked into the pool of light that spilled from the hall.

142

Her face had lost its look of tension. She blinked up at him. "Aren't we going inside?"

He gave a quick grin. "Oh, I don't know, it's rather magical out here with a sweet little witch like you." Nevertheless he carried her into the hallway and set her down. "It's as well you came to me, Adrienne. I'd hate to think of you somewhere else. You're very unusual." He smoothed back her tumbled hair. Adrienne looked up at him and felt the sweet relief wash over her. She had been worried and she didn't care if he knew it. He brushed his hand along her cheek. "I think it's charming to have someone worry about me, Adrienne. It's a long time since anyone did that. Go to bed now, child. Everything's all right."

She smiled at him with quaint formality. "Goodnight, Grant. I'm glad you're home."

The grey eyes that met hers were oddly brilliant. "Run along, little one. Sleep well."

It was only when she had turned out the light that she had remembered he had not told her where he had been.

A few days later Grant flew to Melbourne for a Wool-Growers' Convention. He came into the office to say goodbye. "It's a pity you're not a faded forty," he said ruefully, tracing a finger down her satiny cheek.

Adrienne flew to the defence of the forties and over. "But Grant, some of our . . ."

He held up a hand, his teeth showing very white against his tan. "Adrienne, will you stop! I'm not referring to the forties as being . . . oh, dammit!" He shrugged the whole thing off impatiently. "What I mean, you crazy girl, is I could do with your services in Melbourne, but taking you is out of the question." Adrienne wasn't naïve enough to ask why.

"What a pity, Grant!" She was charmingly sympathetic.

He pulled her to her feet, still smiling, and she lost a little of her colour. "Yes, Adrienne, I'm going to kiss you. Now is the time to scream if you're going to." He tilted her chin, brushing her mouth with his own, lightly at first, then he gathered her close into his arms, his mouth demanding. It was almost as though he couldn't help himself any longer and didn't care much who knew it. He lifted his head, but still held her. She looked a little shaken, as well she might. As a kiss, it was a fairly shattering affair. He waited for her to speak.

"Which one of us is being thrown to the lions?" she managed.

He turned her palm into his mouth and took leave of her, laughing.

Understandably the rest of the week came as an anticlimax. The weekend was a decided improvement. On the Saturday morning Mrs. Manning and Adrienne were relaxing over an iced coffee when a car pulled up in the drive. Adrienne's heart leapt. Joy exploded in her like a rocket. Grant was home!

Mrs. Manning crossed to the window and turned back, an expression of undisguised horror on her face. "My goodness, it's Lyla, and she's got luggage!" She went out into the hall, her face under control. Adrienne heard her greet the uninvited guest. "Lyla darling! I've never been so pleased to see anyone. Are you staying, dear?" Adrienne laughed. The infamy of it! She must have been counting the pieces of luggage.

Adrienne gave them a moment, then went out on to the veranda in time to see the two old friends exchange a kiss of peace or greeting or social custom or whatever it was supposed to be. "Good morning, Mrs. Duncan. May I help you with your luggage?"

Lyla swung around and to Adrienne's dismay advanced on her, arms outstretched in an excess of sisterly love. Adrienne had her face kissed resoundingly. She was a terrible old lady, but you couldn't help liking her. "Not got Grant to marry you, miss?"

Adrienne flinched and Mrs. Manning shook her head warningly over the determinedly pink coiffure. Why, the offensive old thing made it sound like a shotgun affair!

Lyla took over. "Come inside, you two. I've got something to tell you." She didn't believe in standing on ceremony.

The "you two" fell in behind her and Adrienne sidetracked to the kitchen to alert Mrs. Ford. She had no need – Mrs. Ford had her own inbuilt radar. When Adrienne got back to the living room Lyla was holding forth. The cigarette holder was very much in evidence, keeping at bay Mrs. Manning's attempts to talk.

"And that's how I'd do it." She craned her neck at Adrienne. "Fix up about my tea?" Adrienne nodded, Mrs. Ford was on the way.

Mrs. Manning was clutching the beautifully matched pearls around her throat as though they were choking her. "What do you think, Adrienne? Lyla is here to help us out. Isn't that sweet of her? She thinks I'm getting too old to handle it on my own." This time the sarcasm was unmistakable.

Lyla grunted. "You could do with a hand, Helen. It's about time you admitted it."

Helen simmered. It wasn't as though they were contemporaries. The old wretch must be at least eighty. No one seemed to know exactly. She had been around longer than anyone else.

Lyla added fuel to the fire. "You're not as young as you were," she snorted.

Mrs. Manning managed not to wince, but the strain of behaving as a hostess should was beginning to tell on her.

Adrienne rallied behind her. "I think Mrs. Manning has nearly everything organised, haven't you, Mrs. Manning?" She turned to the older woman.

Mrs. Manning nodded faintly, then found her voice. "Well, near enough as not to matter."

Lyla wasn't convinced. This called for team work and she was definitely going to be part of the team. It was a good thing she had run into Aggie Gill. She had a shrewd idea, a hundred per cent correct as it happened, that Helen wasn't going to let her in on it. Another day, and it would have been too late to move in. Lyla sat back and accepted tea from Mrs. Ford. "How's the leg, Nell?"

Mrs. Manning looked around in astonishment, whether at the question or the fact her housekeeper's name was Nell, Adrienne couldn't determine. Mrs. Ford was disposed to be voluble. She seemed genuinely pleased to see Lyla. Mrs. Manning sat back as though the situation was beyond her. She looked across at Adrienne sombrely and, despite every effort, Adrienne laughed. She knew she shouldn't have, but she did.

"Good, that makes two of us," Lyla was saying.

Mrs. Manning broke in pleasantly enough. "Mrs. Duncan will be staying, Mrs. Ford." No Nell for her. "You'll see to everything?" Even the housekeeper's nod was competent. Her burst of enthusiasm, however, had ended. She moved out of the room like a shadow, Adrienne thought, and that wasn't easy for a big woman.

"I might as well tell you I tried to get her," Lyla confessed. "Money no object too," she chortled. The dreadful old thing! Mrs. Manning couldn't remember being so irritated. Lyla was the silliest woman she knew. "Nothing doing," Lyla went on. "She likes it here. Can you beat that?" She laughed, then started to cough, and Mrs. Manning got up and gave her an unnecessarily hard pat on the back. Adrienne wondered with reason how the two old friends would pass the weekend, but strangely enough, after a stormy morning, the atmosphere had cleared by nightfall.

Lyla made sure she lived up to her character part, and told sometimes rude, often funny, stories one after the

146

other at dinner, totally ignoring Mrs. Manning's protestations that Adrienne was too young or she didn't care for such talk. Lyla made no bones about enjoying her own jokes. This evening she had grown tired of the Ringo effect, for she was wearing a magnificent emerald and diamond brooch and matching earrings. Adrienne felt a vague stirring of envy. She knew she would look lovely in those – a lot better than old Lyla!

"Keep your eyes off the jewels, girl. These were given to me by my late husband." She fingered the brooch lovingly and swore lamentably when she pricked her finger on the clasp. Adrienne watched her pick up her fine damask table napkin and proceed to wipe away the speck of blood with a fine disregard for her hostess's linen. A look of malicious pleasure had crossed Mrs. Manning's face when Lyla had drawn blood. Obviously the two old friends enjoyed each other's discomfort.

Taken all round, the evening passed quite happily, and the next day as well. Once you had accepted the fact of Lyla's presence she proved quite entertaining. Mrs. Ford blossomed unexpectedly under her attention, so much so that she fell down heavily in the hall, bringing iced China tea. Adrienne heard the thud and rushed to the housekeeper's assistance. Mrs. Ford looked very white and was lying at a most peculiar angle. Adrienne felt sick. What could she do? She couldn't lift the woman, because she was too heavy. All she could remember was to keep the patient warm. That wasn't too difficult at the height of summer.

"Are you all right, Mrs. Ford?" she solicited inadequately. The poor woman looked dreadful. Why wasn't Grant home? Adrienne thought helplessly. He could lift her. She would have to go for one of the hands.

A fine sweat had broken out on the housekeeper's face. "It's my ankle. I've come down on it."

Adrienne was aghast. She knew she would have to get the shoe off, and fast. Where on earth was Lyla? The old

147

lady walked through in answer to her invocation. "Good grief, Nell, what are you doing on the floor?" she queried with lively curiosity.

She sounded so uncaring that Adrienne snapped back. "Well, she's not dusting!"

"That will do, miss." Lyla came over to have a look and mercifully took charge. Within minutes she had clapped her hands at two startled hands who were sweeping up the poinciana blossoms from the drive; got Mrs. Ford into her bed; the shoe off, the foot up, a tot of brandy administered, and the doctor summoned. Adrienne and Mrs. Manning hovered anxiously in her wake. Mrs. Ford was a better colour, but she was obviously in pain. Doctor Evans arrived and gave his opinion. It coincided with the other's – a bad sprain. He administered a pain-killer and left the patient in Lyla's care. He had seen at once she was the capable one. There she stood by the bedside, a tower of strength.

Mrs. Manning remarked rather uncharitably to Adrienne that it wasn't beyond the realms of possibility that it was part of an organised campaign to get Mrs. Ford, and where had she been at the time of the fall? You couldn't put anything past Lyla. The situation did present a problem, all the same. With the cook laid up there rose the question of her successor.

Mrs. Manning had left no doubt as to her capabilities in that direction. Lyla was, after all, an old lady and wealthy enough never to have touched a saucepan in years. But Lyla surprised them. Mrs. Manning was just sounding Adrienne out in the most devious way possible when Lyla came through to the living room sporting an apron and waving a wooden spoon – her credentials, presumably.

"I hope you girls like Spaghetti Bolognaise à la Duncan, because that's what we're having."

Adrienne was all for it. She loved spaghetti anyway, and à la Duncan might be an improvement. She was rapidly acquiring great faith in Lyla. "Marvellous," she said with some enthusiasm, "with mushrooms and garlic bread?"

"Great heavens, listen to her!" Lyla rolled her eyes, then relented. "Yes, with mushrooms and garlic bread."

Mrs. Manning had been noticeably silent. Lyla fixed her with a hawk eye. "Well, Helen, what do you say?"

Mrs. Manning's face was a complete giveaway. It was quite obvious she thought the meal wouldn't be up to much but she felt obliged to say the right thing. "Yes, of course, Lyla, that's quite all right with me," she managed, with her glance going from one to the other. "If you think you can."

Lyla said a naughty word and went back to the kitchen. Adrienne laughed and followed the rude old thing. She wanted to help – she wasn't a bad cook herself – but Lyla had other ideas. She soon found Adrienne all the interesting little bits like chopping the onion, and crushing the garlic, and tenderly rinsing the cultivated mushrooms. She was such amusing and outrageous company that Adrienne found herself not minding in the least. Dinner was a huge success, and to cap its glory, Mrs. Ford had bitten into the spaghetti and pronounced it *al dente*. She could bestow no higher accolade. Lyla had rifled the wine cellar and clouted on to one of Grant's best clarets. There was no doubt it contributed to the success of the evening. Over coffee and cheesecake, Lyla and her now mellowed hostess launched into plans. Adrienne left them to it.

She called in on Mrs. Ford, who was looking quite alarming in a mauve nightie, to see if there was anything she wanted. The lady said no, but actually there was. She did need a new nightie. Adrienne went straight to her room, feeling a little tired. Washing up wasn't Lyla's forte.

In the week that followed Mrs. Manning had the grace to regret her initial dismay, for Lyla proved a treasure. She had enormous energy even for a woman many years her junior, and was quite frankly enjoying her role of house-keeper, probably because it was scheduled for such a short run; Mrs. Ford was already on the mend. To be strictly fair, it should be mentioned that Adrienne came in for a great deal of the "donkey work" as Lyla liked to call it.

A quick liking had sprung up between the two, so much so that Lyla now lent a hand with the washing up. Adrienne was stacking the dishes back in the cupboard one evening while Lyla sat and watched her. After a while, Adrienne began to whistle the *allegretto* from Beethoven's Seventh Symphony and, to her astonishment, Lyla joined in.

Lyla broke off to say, "I've got a little something for you later, for being a good girl." Adrienne turned round in rare surprise and got waved back to the cupboard. "One of the few instances of virtue being rewarded," Lyla wheezed.

The "little something" turned out to be a pearl dress ring with the largest and loveliest pearl Adrienne had ever seen. She gazed down at it speechless, too embarrassed for words. Surely the reward was out of all proportion to the deeds? "Oh, Lyla," she breathed, "I can't accept this. It's far too valuable!"

"For the love of heaven, get on to her! This day and age and you can't accept it indeed!" She leaned forward urgently. "Take it from me, girl, when a gift is offered, grab it. It doesn't matter who it's from. Grab it. It's the very least you can do."

Adrienne slipped the ring on her finger, feeling like Elizabeth Taylor, and Lyla looked down at it. The girl had beautiful hands; the ring had never looked so well. She had the right skin for pearls. It wasn't often Lyla gave anything away, and she was enjoying the unfamiliar sensation. "Wear it," she ordered. "Pearls are meant to be worn. They keep their lustre that way." She held Adrienne's eye. "I don't know if you're aware of it, girl, but your native land produces the finest cultured pearls in the world." Adrienne wasn't. She imagined Japan did, but she didn't like to say so. Lyla was looking for all the world like the Public Relations Officer for the South Seas Pearling Company.

Lyla took hold of the ring finger with a firm grip. "That one there is a baroque – an irregular shaped one – but even then it's valued at eight hundred and fifty dollars." Adrienne blinked, not only in surprise – Lyla was hurting her finger. The old lady ignored her. She was warming to a favourite subject. "The Japanese cultured pearl is under the half-inch in diameter, ours are from the half-inch to seven-tenths. Most of them are sold on the European markets . . . more lucrative. They can't afford them here." She sniffed disparagingly, then calmly refuted the statement. "I have a chain I'll show you one day. It's valued at a hundred thousand dollars. Some change, eh!" she chuckled.

Adrienne agreed. She couldn't get over the value of her own "little something".

Lyla was pleasantly benign. "If you are interested, I'll show you my opal collection as well." The old nose twitched with pride. "It's quite a collection, I assure you." Adrienne imagined it would be. The shop window had been impressive enough.

Lyla thundered in the manner of the old-time orators, "In them you shall see the living fire of the ruby, the glorious purple of the amethyst, the green sea of the emerald, all glittering together in an incredible mixture of light." Adrienne sat stunned. "Pliny the Elder," Lyla barked. Thank goodness for that! Adrienne had thought it was Lyla.

Mrs. Manning was impressed with the gift when Adrienne showed it to her. Lyla was very generous with her money if only for tax purposes, but she had never heard of her parting with her possessions. She had never given Mrs. Manning, who had housed and fed her on many an occasion, so much as a commemorative spoon.

151

"You must show it to Grant, dear," she murmured admiringly.

Adrienne had every intention of showing it to Grant, but she would have a little joke with him first.

The following Tuesday Lyla and Mrs. Manning went into the town for a committee meeting. They had argued the point all through breakfast, hostilities restored. Adrienne was glad they did not need her for the "spade work" as Lyla put it.

She walked out on to the veranda in time to see Robbie, the chauffeur for the morning, bring the station wagon to the foot of the stairs. This morning the ladies had surpassed themselves. In view of Lyla's predilection for sumptuous dressing, Mrs. Manning had settled for deliberately understated elegance. She couldn't have provided a more perfect foil.

Adrienne came up short. "Why, Lyla, you look . . . gorgeous!" And gorgeous she was in a glitter-melon Thai silk ensemble that made Adrienne feel positively underprivileged.

Lyla preened. "If I say it myself, I'll send them spinning."

Mrs. Manning gave a vinegary smile. "Have you ever thought of a wig, dear?" she asked.

Lyla eyed her with suspicion. "That would be an unnecessary painting of the lily." She settled her turban more firmly on her head and sailed out like a Sultan, her magnificent assurance clear indication of her enormous wealth.

Mrs. Manning gave Adrienne her secret "pearls among swine" look, and Adrienne laughed to herself. The townswomen would have something to talk about tonight! Adrienne saw them off and stayed on the veranda waiting for Chris, who had promised to call over. Not long after, the Holden turned into the drive and Adrienne went down the stairs to greet him.

152

"Good morning, beautiful. The Aston Martin is waiting. Dare I hope you've missed me?"

"I have, Chris." She smiled at him. "Where are we going?"

Chris switched on the ignition. "I thought we'd call over at the Donaldsons'. Tammy seems very taken with you."

"You've seen her, then, Chris?" Adrienne slanted a glance at him.

"Yes, I've been over. I used to go a lot before Rene was married." He laughed out loud. "I was rather keen on Rene at one stage." He turned his head and looked at her. "I soon got over that. Come to think of it, Tammy has come on lately. She looked pretty sharp the other day."

Adrienne smiled to herself and said nothing. Tammy must have taken her advice to heart.

Tammy had. Even Adrienne was surprised. Gone was the jillaroo and in her place a citrus-scented, crisp-cottoned, nicely made-up Tamara. She looked sidelong at Adrienne and winked.

Chris who had missed the wink, looked down at her. "Do you know, Tam, I was just saying to Adrienne how you've come on."

Tammy gave a cool little laugh, nicely off-hand. "Do you think so, Chris?" She turned away with a nice show of indifference to his opinions. Adrienne tried not to laugh. Chris was looking slightly taken back, masculine fashion. Tammy took hold of Adrienne's arm with her best social manner. "Do come in, Adrienne. Mum is dying to meet you." Chris followed the two girls into the house.

Biralee was obviously meant to house children, and there were six in the Donaldson family. The living space had been arranged to suit their lively demands. The main living room was free of toys, but despite the fact that "visitors" were coming, Adrienne had inadvertently trodden on Bugs Bunny in the hall. The older children were at school, but there were still two at home. Adrienne

153

said hello to them; one replied, the other didn't. The youngest was only two, yet he was capable of holding an intelligent conversation over a short period, then he became bored with the whole thing. Children really did come on faster in big families, she thought.

Mrs. Donaldson was a bright attractive little woman, looking much younger than her forty years. Tammy wasn't in the least like her. She must resemble her father, Adrienne thought, and wondered if she would meet the gentleman.

The wallpaper in the living room was rather extraordinary. It featured large-as-life delicious-looking fruit and vegetables. Adrienne couldn't tear her eyes away from it.

"Dad did that. He got it at a sale – he likes it." She laughed good-naturedly.

"It's very attractive, Mrs. Donaldson," Adrienne managed. And so it was.

Tammy came back with morning tea. They had gone to a lot of trouble as all outback people do. Hospitality out West had to be experienced to be believed. Chris tucked in, though it couldn't be that long since he had had his breakfast. Everything was homemade – the cakes, the scones, the biscuits, the butter, the jam, the scalded cream. It was delicious. Adrienne said so.

"I'm glad you like it, dear. Though none of us are up to Nell Ford." Mrs. Donaldson fell into reminiscences of some of Mrs. Ford's greatest public culinary feats for the district. The only thing the townswomen had against her was that she would never part with a recipe, even for marmalade.

"Show Chris the new separator, love." She turned to her daughter. Adrienne could see from the maternal light in her eye that she was forwarding the match. Tammy deigned to do so with a pretty show if reluctance. Mrs. Donaldson waited until they were safely out of earshot, then remarked proudly, "My little Tammy's a good girl.

154

She'll make Chris a good wife, mark my words." She spoke as if it was a foregone conclusion. Adrienne hoped for everyone's sake that they could mark them. These mothers were the matchmaking end!

Adrienne was shown around the house while Mrs. Donaldson kept up a light cheerful conversation. She looked the visitor over well and truly, though Adrienne let her think she was unaware of it. Mrs. Donaldson was painfully anxious to protect her daughter's interests. Fortunately for Adrienne she appeared quite satisfied with her intentions.

The two of them watched Chris and Tammy come back to the house from the shade of the veranda. Tammy was looking more vivacious and Chris seemed to be responding favourably. It was all Adrienne could do not to laugh at the combined mother-daughter effort. Chris didn't have a show. Though it was clear Tammy would, as her mother put, "Make him a good wife," it did seem a little cold-blooded.

"She sure knows her way around a piece of machinery," Chris informed them seriously, with an admiring glance at Tammy. Evidently the trip to the cowshed had borne results, Adrienne thought.

They stayed for lunch, although the men of the house did not appear, and about one o'clock they waved their goodbyes. Tammy had asked Adrienne's advice regarding a ball dress – the word had spread. Everyone knew of Mrs. Manning's latest and most spectacular event. Adrienne had promised to work on it. She rather thought one of her own would suit Tammy.

On the way back they called in on Careewa. Marion, who was a talented artist, was busy on some posters to advertise the grand affair. Adrienne looked over her shoulder. They were charming and most original. "Do you do much of this sort of thing, Marion?" she asked.

"On and off, dear. I had four years' training before I was married." She got up and hunted through a cupboard and came back with a well-stuffed portfolio. In it were sketches of everyone – Chris, Grant, Mrs. Manning, Mrs. Ford rising from the stove like an Aphrodite, old Mee Lee, the gardener; lots of faces unfamiliar to Adrienne and dozens of sketches of flowers and trees. They were remarkably good likenesses of the people Adrienne knew and the other drawings, especially the flowers were quite beautiful. Adrienne was impressed.

"May I take these, Marion, and have a good look at them?" They were well worth spending time over.

"Of course, dear, though there's nothing much there." Marion dismissed the sketches with a negligent wave of her hand.

Adrienne didn't agree. She thought Marion possessed considerable talent. She was certain there would be work for her as an illustrator. A woman needed something creative to do. Really, Marion was wasted out here! Adrienne found herself echoing Mrs. Manning.

Then an idea occurred to her. "Why don't you incorporate the jacarandas into the posters, Marion? Mrs. Donaldson was saying they're nearly synonymous with Saranga."

Marion gave it a moment's consideration. "That's not a bad idea. I don't know why I didn't think of it myself. We'll go one better and have a spray of jacaranda on the official invitations." Her artistic eye lit up. She was already sketching in her head.

Chris laughed. "We'll leave you to it, Mum. I'll get Adrienne back to the house."

Marion came down to the car with them. "Tell Helen about the jacaranda idea, Adrienne. I think she'll be pleased." She waved them off and went back inside the house feeling pleasurably inspired. Of course, the jacaranda! Why not the jacaranda? People had been known to drive miles out to Saranga just to see them in bloom. Trust Adrienne to come up with it. She was a very bright girl and a most accomplished pianist, so Helen was

156

saying. Marion cleared the old sketches off the drawing board and got down to work.

By their look of unaccustomed accord, Mrs. Manning and Lyla had had a good day. They were enthusiastic about the jacaranda motif too.

Lyla was disposed to tell lies. "I must say I thought of it myself," she remarked quite blandly. Mrs. Manning arched a delicate eyebrow, but said nothing. That Lyla was the biggest liar she knew!

Late the next afternoon Adrienne walked down the drive to look at her brain-children. A musky breeze whirled about her head and in the chirruping shade lurked a hundred birds. Mee Lee must have been burning off somewhere, for there was a sweet puff of burning gum tips on the air. She turned the bend in the drive and the jacarandas came into shape, spirit trees filigreed against the pink and gold of the setting sun.

Poetry came into her head. She walked along reciting out loud.

"In the golden light of the setting sun
The pale purple even melts around thy flight
Like a glow-worm golden in a dell of dew
What leaf-fringed legend haunts about thy shape
Forlorn! The very word is like a bell."

Bell! What a lovely word! The purple blue bells of the jacaranda crunched under her feet. Jacaranda time! Such a short time, yet long enough to fall in love. She had missed Grant unbearably. Some days there didn't seem any point in getting up. There was a great space in her waiting to be filled with love – Grant's love. "I'll have to do something about this," Adrienne said out loud, "but I can't think what."

A butterfly alighted on her shoulder in need of companionship. He clung, then folded, then fluttered out his bright banner. Adrienne kept quite still. She loved this place. It gave her a feeling of belonging. The butterfly flew off. Adrienne shut her eyes tight and wished for Grant. Not far off was the sound of a car horn. Her eyes flew open, startled at the extent of her own powers.

That was the Mercedes. Ecstatic little shivers started at the base of her neck and tickled their way up into her head. This was awful – she was going to pieces. And she wasn't wearing her ring! Perhaps it was just as well. Grant might offer his best wishes and that would be that. On the other hand she would know where she stood. As it was, she stood rooted to the spot, and Grant braked a few feet away. He swung out of the car – the same Grant, tall, dark and incredibly dear. Adrienne was so pleased to see him that she offered him her hand, much as she would the merest acquaintance.

Grant laughed and took it, but instead of shaking it he carried it to his lips. "Penelope, you quaint child," he murmured. His eyes held the same lazy indulgence. Adrienne was dismayed. Penelope! Who was Penelope? She quite missed the reference. Grant watched the expressions chase across her evanescent little face. "Penelope, my love, waited for Ulysses!"

Adrienne felt the need to put him in his place. "I wasn't waiting for you, Ulysses. I was looking at the jacaranda."

Grant put an arm around her shoulders and led her to the car. "My hopes are dashed." He didn't seem upset by it at all.

Adrienne watched him in the rear vision as he crossed round the back of the car. He was smiling. He looked depressingly handsome and confident. Adrienne withdrew to her corner. "Quaint child!" Surely a man didn't call the woman he loved a quaint child. It didn't seem likely. Though he hadn't kissed her like a child. Definitely not! Even that meant nothing. Only the other day a Minister had been forced to resign for kissing the office girl. The Minister probably thought she was a quaint child.

Grant turned to look at her. "What is it, Adrienne?"

She said what she was thinking. "I see where a Minister has resigned for kissing the office girl."

Grant followed her line of thought entirely. "Oh, Adrienne," he groaned, and pulled her into his arms. She didn't think to resist. Grant lifted her head. "It's a good thing I can't be called on to resign!"

She offered a small protest. "I don't think I can continue as your secretary, Grant."

He laughed and tucked back her tumbled hair. "Well, continue as a little friend of the family, then."

This was no good. They were unevenly matched – he was running rings around her. She sighed and told him about the jacarandas and Marion's posters.

Grant listened politely and then turned her to face him, holding her hand in his own. "I've got some news of my own. I called in on your father on the way back."

Adrienne couldn't have been more surprised. "You what!"

Her tone was so frankly disbelieving that Grant laughed. "As old Mee Lee picturesquely puts it, I don't boil my cabbages twice."

"Gracious, are you serious, Grant?"

"Of course I am, my dear. Why ever not? Your father would like to know his only daughter is in good hands." He started to laugh.

Adrienne ignored him. Fancy Grant calling in to see her father! What on earth for? "Did you meet Linda?" she asked dryly.

Grant looked straight ahead. "As a matter of fact, I did. I had dinner with them. Your father wouldn't hear of anything else. I liked him." He turned to her. "I might as well tell you so you won't go brooding about it on your own; your stepmother is expecting a baby."

It was Adrienne's day for surprises. "A what?" she gasped. "How disgusting!"

Grant gave her his full attention, his look a censure.

"What an extraordinary thing to say, Adrienne. Your stepmother is blooming and your father is understandably pleased about it. He would like a son, someone to carry on the business, quite apart from anything else."

"Son be bothered!" To her intense mortification, Adrienne started to cry. She put her hands over her face and cried like a small child, and as broken-heartedly. That was the end of her. She would never be wanted at home now. Linda and her son would see to that. How fickle men were! Her father was pleased, was he! He ought to be ashamed of himself. She was reacting rather badly.

Grant watched her for a moment in silence, then pulled her hands down from her face, reached for his pocket handkerchief and tenderly and efficiently wiped away all traces of tears. "That's enough now, sweetheart. You're a big girl, remember."

Adrienne gazed back at him mournfully, her eyes deep and drowning. "That's the death knell for me, you know," she said dramatically.

Despite himself, Grant laughed. "Don't be absurd! Your father loves you dearly. No one could replace his little girl. But life goes on, Adrienne, and your father is entitled to his slice of it. You can't expect him to live it your way. However much you may resent Linda, she is making your father happy. She's very much in love with him, and no wonder. He's a very striking-looking man." He looked at her critically. "You don't resemble him in any way, do you? It would have been easier for you if you had; with Linda, I mean. I'm a bit like you, I'm afraid – I didn't like her, although she went all out to be charming."

Adrienne stared at him in silence. Shock was reacting on her. She would have a little stepbrother the living spit of Linda. "Into the valley of death rode the six hundred," she whispered.

Grant held up her chin and laughed. "I suppose I should be used to you, but I'm not. What on earth has that got to do with it?"

Adrienne looked at him. "I always say that when things go wrong. It helps me triumph over adversity."

Grant brushed her mouth with his own. "I think you've lost a few men, sweetheart." He switched on the ignition and took the car up the drive. She was wrong about her father. He had never stopped singing his daughter's praises. It was then that Grant had noticed the hard core in Linda. She was a very possessive woman, and he had definitely not liked her. It was as well Adrienne was away from her.

After dinner, Grant had some presents to find out. He always brought something back from his trips. Even Lyla came in for one. "What is it, dear boy? A naked woman in bronze?" It wasn't – only a rather interesting opal from Altmann and Cherny, Lyla gloated over it.

Mrs. Manning took an exquisite tea-set in her stride, but Adrienne was overwhelmed by her earrings. They were a delicate perfection of jade and gold, pendant-shaped. Grant wanted to see them on. "I remembered the ones you wore at the barbecue. I liked the style on you then."

Adrienne walked over to the Venetian mirror and adjusted them. Grant came behind her and gathered her hair back on to her nape for a better effect. She turned to him and old Lyla was stopped in her tracks. Mrs. Manning fixed her with such a look of violence that for once the old lady was quiet. There was not the slightest shadow of doubt that Adrienne had lost her heart to Grant. It was on her face for all to see. And why not? He was a handsome devil and charming too, not to mention Saranga. Lyla decided to hold her peace – Helen looked quite fierce.

Adrienne kept her letter from her father until bedtime. She wasn't ready to face up to the "wonderful news" before then. Grant had brought with him the big box containing the ball gown she had asked her father to send; her own creation and a green one she thought would suit

161

Tammy. Grant *was* right. Her father was thrilled with the idea of becoming a father at forty-eight. As Grant put it, he would dearly love a son to carry on the business he had worked so hard to establish. Oh dear! Adrienne felt the tears coming. It was a very loving letter. At the bottom was a postscript.

"I was very impressed with Grant Manning — a man of intelligence and integrity. Of course he would have to have what it takes to have achieved so much and still such a young man. By the way, my little daughter, he's also extremely good-looking, so watch it. I thought you might like a new gown for the big affair, so I've enclosed it along with one for your friend. Be a good girl. I know you're in good hands. This brings all my love. Father.
P.P.S. Do try and drop a note to Linda — anything will do. The baby may take after me."

Adrienne put down her letter and repeated aloud, "The baby may take after Father, the baby may take after Father, the baby may take after Father," much in the way of the Persians renouncing a wife and mother. She felt a lot better. Boy babies did have a way of taking after their fathers.

She swung the box on to the bed excitedly and cut through the string with her nail scissors. Masses of tissue paper greeted her. The green dress was on top. She lifted it out quickly, not even bothering to hang it up. Gracious, what sumptuous splendour! Her father had perfect taste. Shimmering under her eyes was an opulent shaft of white satin, the Empire bodice aglitter with beads and brilliants, pearls and crystal dewdrops. Oh, she would look a dream in this! Adrienne held the gown up against her and waltzed about the room. Heavens, what had fallen on the carpet? She bent and retrieved it. Beautiful baroque earrings swathed in tissue paper, to match the brilliants in her gown. Good gracious! They were from Linda. Well, they did say pregnancy had a fantastic effect upon women.

162

"Have a lovely, lovely time." Yes, that sounded like Linda. Adrienne tried them on. They were extremely becoming. She felt almost as excited as if it were the very night of the ball.

She examined the green gown carefully. It had been a favourite, and would suit Tammy – pale green glistening marquisette strewn all over with mother-of-pearl roses. Tammy would be pleased. Oh, why, oh, why had she forgotten her evening shoes? Adrienne turned back to the box. Her father couldn't have thought of them, could he? But he had. No wonder he was so successful at business! Tammy would have to find the right shoes for the green. It was important. Maybe they would have something suitable in the town.

Adrienne hung both dresses away and prepared for bed. She picked up things from the dressing table and put them down in the most indeterminate way, as though she had lost track of what she was doing, as indeed she had. She was actually dressing for the ball. She would float down the stairs . . . What a pity there weren't any stairs; you really needed a staircase for romantic effect . . . Grant would be standing at the bottom, his face entranced. "This is what I've been waiting for all my life, this beautiful child."

Adrienne shook out her nightgown and put it on. She was smiling slightly at the undisguised expression of adoration on Grant's face. She turned out the light and stood at the open window. A young moon hung low above the tops of the poinciana. The air was laden with the scents of the garden. She hopped into bed and sang over one of Delilah's songs to herself; a song of undulating love. It quite lulled her to sleep.

CHAPTER NINE

THE following Wednesday Adrienne went into the town with Mrs. Manning and Lyla. It promised to be a blazingly hot day, and all three women dressed to beat it. Robbie drove them in, Adrienne in the front beside him.

The scenery was as heart-warming as ever. They drove through the serenely beautiful avenue of poplars allowing glimpses of the great blue-coloured mountains beyond them.

"Why is it I imagined the outback to be flat?" Adrienne remarked, as much to herself as anyone else.

"Quite common, my dear," Lyla answered for all of them. "In actual fact, we have every sort of climate and scenery one can think of in Australia – enormous stretches of desert, alpine sports, the English countryside in some parts of Victoria, the finest surfing beaches in the world, thousands of miles of your flat veldt country and hills as rugged as any you'd find in Scotland."

"Speaking of hills," Robbie broke into the conversation, "this is a bonzer little hill-climber." He patted the wheel of the station wagon lovingly.

Adrienne smiled at his sidetracking. "Bonzer as in 'you beaut', Robbie?"

"The very same," he winked at her. This Adrienne was some looker, he thought.

In town, Marion's posters were up everywhere. The Manning Memorial Hall was a beehive of women. The swarm broke up at the appearance of their leader. Mrs. Manning opened the meeting. Lyla was at her garrulous best. She kept up a continuous counterpart to the Chairlady's theme. Adrienne enjoyed herself immensely. For once, apart from Lyla, who felt morally obliged to, there was no dissention among the women. Work had already begun on the Government subsidised project and the townswomen were happy. The coming affair was eagerly looked forward to. Mrs. Manning had pulled off another grand slam. It was expected to draw crowds from hundreds of miles around. Some of the women had sons or husbands who would be the amateur jockeys, others owned the winning nags and everyone had placed bets in advance. Three of the local councillors were to act as "bookies", the only difference being that the bag had to be handed over to the Committee.

Adrienne slipped away towards the end of the meeting. She had a few purchases to make. She was just coming out of the main store, her head down counting her change — the assitant hadn't looked too bright — when she almost collided with Vera. Vera! She had hoped never to lay eyes on her again.

"Well, if it isn't Miss Bright Eyes!" A few heads turned. Vera had a very carrying voice. She grasped Adrienne's arm and steered her out into the foyer, and Adrienne felt the pleasure of the morning draining out of her. It left a sick, hollow feeling in her stomach. Anything Vera would have to say would be unpleasant, she was that sort of person.

"I must say, Vera, you have a splendid hide."

Vera looked like a spitting cat, her eyes feline with spite. "Oh, don't make me sick, you little upstart. Did you expect me to hide?"

"Knowing you, no. In any case, I can't stand here swopping unpleasantries with you." Adrienne moved back. "I don't want to discuss our little escapade, if that's what's bothering you."

Vera put out a restraining hand. Her manner was calmer. "Don't be like me, Doll Face. Grant is after Prue Gowan."

Her thrust drove home cleanly. Adrienne lost colour. Prue Gowan! Anyone who ever read the society pages knew of Prue Gowan. She was the heiress to a meat-packing fortune and not a bad-looking girl either.

165

Adrienne spoke from her shell. "It's scarcely my business who Grant is after, as you so crudely put it."

The green eyes flickered. "Well, you're the lucky one. He's been seeing a lot of her lately – Dad told me. A little business mixed with pleasure, was the way he put it."

In the heat of the day Adrienne felt cold. Poor miserable me, I'm dazed, she thought. She looked full into the other girl's eyes. Vera was looking drawn about the nose and mouth. Suddenly Adrienne felt sorry for her as well as for herself. "Don't upset yourself any more, Vera. I'm sorry for your sake that Grant couldn't love you, but you're not very lovable, are you? Why don't you work on it and maybe somebody will?"

She sidestepped the other girl, leaving her standing. She couldn't have managed another word anyway. Her sandals clicked out on the blistering pavement. "Prue Gowan. Prue Gowan." A feeling of depression attacked her. She saw herself a hopelessly poor judge of men and situations. She was a stupid, romantic, inexperienced idiot who had allowed her reason to succumb to a few kisses. Well, quite a few, actually. No matter. She had to break off in her thoughts to murmur, "*Donner und Blitzen!*"

A passing truck driver beeped the horn at her. It wasn't every day you saw a good-looking girl remonstrating with herself in broad daylight. Now she could see the silliness of all her daydreams. She was a pitiable thing like poor Vera. "The moving finger writes and having writ moves on." "Out, damned spot!" she cried aloud.

An old man stopped in his tracks. "That's the lass, that's the lass. Give it to them!"

Adrienne came back to her surroundings. She gave the old fellow a rather strange smile. She would have to put the whole thing out of her head until she was alone, otherwise she might be arrested. "Nor all your tears wash out a line of it," she thought.

Adrienne walked headlong into Mrs. Manning and

Lyla. The meeting was over, and Lyla had decided to drive. She couldn't face the trip back in third gear, which was Mrs. Manning's favourite position. They got home in record time. How Lyla ever managed to hold a licence suggested a little corruption in the traffic department. Not that Adrienne cared – she wouldn't have noticed if they came home in a balloon.

Grant was not in to dinner, and she was thankful for that. She couldn't have faced him. She was in retreat. Mrs. Manning and Lyla did not appear to notice her abstraction, but chatted away like a couple of jangling jam bottles. She wasn't the first to think a man in love with her. It was a case of love believing the unbelievable, love ignoring reality. She had sold her reputation for a song. "Who was that lady I saw you with last night?" No wonder it was an all-time joke, it was true! What a goat she was! "Eek!" she said aloud, her breath rasping with anguish.

Lyla peered over at her. "Whatever is up, girl, you've been squirming over there all night as if you've got ants in your pants."

So much for their not noticing! The rude old thing! What an awful expression! "I've got a few things on my mind," she explained carefully.

"Well, they don't sound too cheerful," Lyla retorted.

Mrs. Manning suggested a second helping of the Cherries Jubilee, but Adrienne didn't feel festive. She excused herself from the table. She felt dreadful. They would not have an inkling of the tears stored up in her. They would be sorry for her if they did. They would never see her tears, they were falling down her heart. "A pity beyond all telling is hid in the heart of love." She went to the piano and played. After a while she wandered into one of her favouitre fragments, the Chopin Fourth Etude. It fitted her mood of melancholia exactly.

"My goodness, there's a dirge!" Lyla had brought her coffee through.

"Oh no, Lyla, it's a most beautiful piece."

167

"To you, miss. I'm not all that soulful. Let's hear some Strauss."

Adrienne launched into the *Blue Danube*. The only rewarding thing about it was its special arrangement. Lyla liked it. After about twenty minutes of waltz time, the older ladies retired, having tired themselves out talking. Adrienne couldn't relax. She felt poisoned or stabbed. She couldn't even read a book. She had to recline in an armchair and stare at the stereogram. After a while she got up and put on a record – the Khachaturian Violin Concerto. The tumultuous opening subdued her, so much so that she drifted away from the intensity of the present.

"Ah, love, could we not shatter it to bits, and then remould it nearer to the heart's desire!" What did he think he was doing, stamping on her heart? She could see herself breaking up into tiny pieces. Her father had said Grant was a man of integrity. Well, men of integrity should be more careful where they put their feet! "Tread softly, because you tread upon my dreams." The violin wailed and throbbed, then leapt in a clean melodic line. Adrienne's jaw tightened. "The nightingale that in the branches sang, ah, whence and whither flown again who knows?" The tears coursed down her cheeks in a torment.

"What are you doing, you ridiculous child?"

Heavens, it was Grant! She made a tremendous effort to control herself. She got up and turned her back to him.

Grant smiled at the vulnerable set of her shoulders. He gave her a moment, then sank down in the chair. "Am I tired!" he sighed.

To admit it, the wicked wanton deceiver! She felt calmer. This was relief. A girl had her pride, after all. He was unscrupulous . . . unworthy.

"Adrienne?" Grant wanted to see her face. She made to swirl past him, but with one twist he had her down in his arms. Adrienne shut her eyes. He must not notice anything odd. She went rigid, and Grant smiled. "Are you going to open your eyes, you mystifying child?"

"My heart at thy sweet voice." She couldn't do much reasoning here. She would have to get up. She struggled and was done for. She fought up from the whirlpool. Another minute and she would vanish into Grant forever. Lightning was flashing in front of her eyes. She hurled a bolt at him: "You're going the right way for the fiery fork!" The dark eyes were fury-bright as she turned on her heel and fled from the room.

After a fitful night of philosophic speculation, Adrienne decided not to resign. Taken as a premise, man was a polygamous animal. It seemed logical to assume that a bird in the hand had more show than one in the city. Why should she fret about tomorrow if today be sweet? Life was one long foolish fret about tomorrow. Yet who could guarantee a tomorrow? It was just as well to hoard up memories like a squirrel. Perhaps no one was meant to be at peace or rest. Uncertainty was a stimulation, a source of endless fascination. That was where she had gone wrong — Grant was too sure of her. Here he was kissing her head-long when he should have led up to it. She should have distributed her kisses like so many rare jewels seldom chanced upon, instead of tipping the bag load in front of him.

The tears tickled her eyelids. Woman was losing her mystery. She was stripped of her fascination, publicly and privately, till there was nothing left to know. You couldn't pick up the newspaper that there wasn't a double section of cavorting females held up and in by the foundation garments to end all foundation garments. Her father had once said that there was nothing sexier than a beautifully-dressed woman, and he should know. Once a woman's charms could only be guessed at: now there was nothing left to know. She was a product of her generation, hellbent on revealing all. By morning she had determined on a course of companionable detachment.

Marion's dormant but ever-present creative urge had become stimulated by Adrienne's very genuine interest, so much so that she had persuaded Adrienne to sit for her.

Like everyone of ability, Marion knew she possessed something more than moderate talent. Her early marriage – she had been married at nineteen – had been the turning point that had taken her out of her sphere of interest. Not that she was unable to paint out here, but she had always depended to a large degree on appreciation and encouragment. She had had that in plenty at art school. Her teachers had assured her of her promise, but life had taken a different turning. She had been so young and so much in love, and Tom had been such fun to be with. But she had matured and so had he. They had many happy days, but they just failed to achieve an intellectual harmony. Tom had been first and last a countryman, his interests almost exclusively to his family and his property. She had missed the atmosphere of her parents' home. They too had been landed people; their home had been the bush, but their interests had been the world. Her parents had been a splendidly matched pair. It was the talk that Marion had missed, the discussions, the arguments, the quality of the conversation. In the early days when she had failed to grasp Tom's complete lack of interest in any art form, she had shown him her drawings and he had said, "Very nice, love," and changed the subject. It would have been the same if she had produced a masterpiece. It was not Tom's fault, nor had it been her own. It was simply a lack of common ground outside their home. Her work had fallen by the wayside. She had devoted her life to Chris and he was a son that any mother would be proud of, but in many ways he was Tom all over again. That was one reason she had never encouraged his interest in Adrienne. Not that she had any need to be anxious, for it was clear that Adrienne had only a fondness for Chris.

The ideal match would be Adrienne and Grant. Her

mood lightened when she thought of Grant. What a strength he had been to her, and he hardly more than a boy. Grant was someone very special. He was a man, a real man, yet he had an empathy for women. You could talk to Grant, pour out your heart to him and rely on his instinctive understanding. If you said the same thing to Chris, he would turn and look at you with a "Come off it, Mum," and you would laugh at his resemblance to Tom. Yes, Grant was a very special person, as near to being a complete human being as Marion had ever met. He would appreciate Adrienne. His personality would complement hers and they would grow together. Strange how they had all become so fond of Adrienne in such a short time. She fitted into the family as if she were one of them. Quite apart from being so lovely, she had a quality of sensitivity and compassion that Marion hoped to capture.

It was some time since she had worked in oils, and she was quite excited about it. They should be here soon. Chris had gone into the town to pick up the two girls, Adrienne and Tammy, after their shopping expedition. About eleven o'clock all three of them hurried up the front stairs. Marion went out to greet them. It was very pleasant, having the young people about her. She smiled at the two girls, "How did it go?"

"A most successful morning's shopping, wouldn't you say, Tam?" Adrienne followed Marion into the house. "We must show you."

"I should hope so. I'm all agog!"

The shoes, the gloves, the entire new make-up kit, all came in for its share of admiration. Tammy had every intention of laying them in the aisles. She went out to the car and came back with the boxed evening gown. "Adrienne has been super. She lent it to me. You want to see it?" Tammy dismissed Chris from the room and held up the gown reverently. Adrienne had been right, the green did suit her, heightening her russet colouring. The new make-up would cover the freckles nicely – not that

171

they needed covering, Adrienne thought. They were rather charming and essentially Tammy, but she seemed to detest them, so they had to be covered at all costs.

Tammy was attaching a great deal of importance to her appearance at the ball and its romantic effect on Chris. Adrienne hoped she would have no cause for disappointment. Everyone was going with the exception of Mrs. Ford and old Mee Lee. Neither of them held with dancing, although Mrs. Ford was more tolerant of others' weaknesses than the old gardener. He had always preferred a rake to a woman. You knew where you were in the garden.

After lunch Chris ran Tammy back to Biralee and Adrienne had her first sitting. Marion was not disposed to talk. She looked different, Adrienne thought. She was always attractive and vivacious, but now she looked blazingly alive and intent.

Adrienne sat through the long preliminary sketchings. She asked no questions. Marion would paint her as she saw her. She was extremely interested in the result. Marion was absorbed, for she had a good subject. The hands were especially interesting and she sketched them rapidly. As yet, she was only searching out ideas. She had no actual pose in mind. That would come. The time flew.

"Dare I intrude upon the sitting?" Adrienne looked across the room straight into the cool grey eyes.

"Grant, darling, how lovely to see you!" Marion put down her charcoal and went over to him. Adrienne watched that mouth brush Marion's cheek.

"It's good to see you working." He went around to the back of the easel. "Hmm, the eyes and the mouth, the poetry and the passion – the hands, yes, you should paint her at the piano turning away from the keyboard. Come over for dinner tonight and see what you think." He ran an affectionate hand over Marion's dark head. "You look happy, my dear."

"I am, Grant. If this is any good, and I feel that it might be, I intend to enter it for the Casson Prize, just as an

172

interest." Marion turned to Adrienne. "With your permission, of course, my dear."

Adrienne looked from one to the other. "I would be honoured, Marion."

Grant had not addressed one word to her.

"We're just going to have coffee, Grant. You'll have some?"

Grant nodded lazily and Marion went through to the kitchen. "Aren't we speaking, Miss Brent?"

"I usually speak when I'm spoken to, Mr. Manning."

Grant laughed. "If that were only true! Come over here."

Adrienne declined the invitation. She had gone weak at the knees anyhow. "Marion is wasted out here," she said.

Grant frowned. "I don't like that 'out here', Adrienne. An artist can paint anywhere. In any case, it's very beautiful out here through the change of the seasons, though Marion's speciality is portraiture. What Marion lacks is the driving force, the impetus necessary for any art form to thrive. It might have been different if Tom had been more appreciative of her gift." Grant delved for a cigarette. "I'll admit that life would be far more stimulating to her as an artist in the city, but it was her wish to stay out here, you know. When Chris marries, I think she'll move in with my Aunt Sara. Sara will get her going if anyone will – probably married off as well." The grey eyes were very level. "Would 'out here', as you put it, be so bad, Adrienne?"

Adrienne felt like screaming. There he was, at it again, making those devious remarks! She wanted to cry out like the heroine of an old-fashioned melodrama, "Declare yourself, declare yourself! Make known your dishonourable intentions!" But of course he wasn't going to.

"No answer, I see." Grant looked over his shoulder. Marion was coming back.

"I think we'll have it out on the terrace. It's so much cooler." She led the way to the back of the house. It faced the mountains.

173

Adrienne was enchanted. "Why, Marion, what a bliss-ful retreat!" She stepped out on to the terrace and took a deep breath of the mild mountain air. Three flowering peaches threw shade over the flagstones and a feathery Japanese maple guarded the edge of a small ornamental pool. Around the pool grew iris and daphne and verbenas, watched over by late-flowering azaleas in tubs. An umbrella-shaped albizzia spread its silky pink bristles towards the flowering wilderness.

Marion smiled. "Shall we tell her who planned it?"

Grant poured the coffee. "I don't see why not. I'm out to impress." He drew up the wrought-iron chairs. "With my own two hands I established this Eden." His gaze at Adrienne was sardonic as if he expected instant incredul-ity.

She surprised him with her total admiration. "It's lovely, Grant, absolutely lovely." She turned her face towards to the maple.

> *"Come sit aneath this maple,*
> *Whose lofty tressed crown*
> *Sighs, as her tufty sprays stir*
> *To the west wind's kiss:*
> *And with the babbling waters*
> *My flute thy care shall drown*
> *And lull thy dreamy eyelids to sweet*
> *   forgetful bliss."*

"I don't know that, Adrienne. Whose is it?" Marion was studying her rapt expression with an artist's eye.

Adrienne came down to earth. "I don't know, to be honest. I have an idea it's Plato. In any case, it was a pine tree."

Grant made a face. "Such staggering erudition! Have your coffee, child. It's going cold."

Adrienne smiled at them. "I used to write poetry once – reams of it, fearful stuff. I got a prize once. What was it?

'On either side the river lie'."

Grant laughed. "You didn't write that!"

"No, of course not. Something like that. I know –

A soft white mist the river kissed
Moved to the trees and settled.
Only the breeze a gossmer tease
Nudged the moonstruck petals'."

Grant looked at Marion, his mouth indulgent. "Are we to understand she got a prize for that?"

"I was only about twelve, Grant." Adrienne sounded apologetic.

"Well, that's not so very long ago, is it?" His smile sharpened. "You're wasted out here."

They chatted amiably through afternoon tea, then Marion went out to the car with them to see them off. "Chris and I will be over about seven. Until then—" She stood back from the car and waved them off.

Adrienne edged back in her corner, feeling desperately unsettled. "I didn't say goodbye to Chris," she said reproachfully.

"Well, you'll have another opportunity tonight, my love."

"I don't know why you say that, Grant."

"Say what, sweet Adrienne?"

Adrienne made a sound of annoyance and looked out the window. She just wasn't sophisticated enough for him. Maybe that was what he liked in Prue Gowan. "I saw Vera in town last week," she said.

Grant took his eyes off the road for an instant. "Did you now? That's enlightening."

"I'm just trying to make conversation, Grant. You're being rather difficult."

Grant laughed. Adrienne could not even bring herself to mention Prue Gowan's name. Adrienne tried again. "Are you coming to the ball, Grant?"

"My dear, I shall claim every dance."

"I don't think you'll be able to. I expect to look ravishing that night."

Grant laughed. "Well, I'm inviting a few friends from Sydney, so perhaps the other ladies will take pity on me."

Adrienne's heart sank. "A party of friends. . . ." That was all she needed to know. She maintained a brave front. "Well, I certainly hope so, for your sake."

The grey eyes were alight with laughter. "Oh, stop it, baby, you're ridiculous!"

Adrienne subsided. She was in anguish. If only she could bear up until she was in her room! She did. In fact the family had never seen her so vivacious as she was that evening. Though she hated herself afterwards, she even flirted with Chris. That was her smarting heart.

Marion saw Grant's point about using the piano when she played for them after dinner. Adrienne had an undeniable affinity for the keyboard. Marion toyed over the idea in her head. Grant unobtrusively handed her some blank sheets and a drawing pencil and she made some lightning sketches. Lyla was intrigued. She had often thought hers was a face for the canvas.

When Adrienne had finished playing she said just that to Marion. "If you want to paint a real face get on to mine." She turned her head and jutted her chin.

Marion laughed. "I don't know if I could capture the essential you, Lyla. Your face is so . . . so mobile."

Mrs. Manning almost sniffed. "Mobile" was certainly the diplomatic word!

"If this painting is up to the mark, I'm thinking of entering it for the Casson Prize," Marion went on.

"Good grief!" Lyla was thrilled. "Well, you couldn't do better than paint me. Everyone knows me and I have very real character in my face. It's all those lines, you don't get them for nothing. Of course I was a beauty as a girl," she tossed off. This was a downright outrageous lie. If anything, she had improved over the years.

176

The artist was a trifle disconcerted. "I would be pleased to paint you, Lyla, but it would be easier for me at this stage to start with Adrienne and work up to you. I haven't done any serious work for years."

Lyla leant forward. "My dear, anyone, but anyone, can paint a young girl. It takes a master to put my face on canvas."

"You said it," Mrs. Manning retorted over-loud.

"What's that, Helen?" Lyla turned on her friend.

"I say, my dear, I couldn't agree with you more. I think it would be better for Marion to try her hand with Adrienne." She turned to Grant. "Could you mix me a Martini, dear, and one for you girls?" The conversation was skilfully deflected.

Not to be put off, Chris had brought over some of his own records. "Shall We Dance?" fell on the turntable and he turned to Adrienne. "I promise to do a little better than the King of Siam." Adrienne smiled into his mesmerised eyes and he opened the french windows leading out on to the veranda.

Lyla couldn't resist a parting sally. "We're keeping an eye on you!"

Mrs. Manning shut her eyes briefly. "That will not be necessary, Lyla." Lyla snorted.

Outside on the veranda, Adrienne made-believe she was dancing with Grant. But even with her imagination it didn't work out. Chris was not his cousin. It wasn't fair to any of them. They drifted down to the end of the veranda where the moonlight fell softly through the vines. The leaves swished gently, revealing a cobweb transformed into a brilliant thing, a shimmer of silvery thread.

Chris's arms tightened about her. "Gosh, you're lovely, Adrienne."

"Chris!" There was a faint plea in her voice and he heard it.

He sighed. "You're not with me, sweetheart, are you?"

"I'm very fond of you, Chris, you know that." She

177

lifted her hand and patted his cheek and he turned his mouth into the palm.

"You can't win 'em all," he joked, and looked out over the flame tree, aware of her face with its look of tenderness.

"I'm sorry, Chris," she said involuntarily.

He smiled at her. "What for, dark eyes? For being so beautiful?"

Grant strolled out on to the veranda. "My dear children, if you don't want Lyla out here with a searchlight, you'd better come in."

Chris laughed. "I'll fix her. I'll ask for a dance," He did and regretted it. Lyla loved dancing.

They had a late evening.

Adrienne couldn't sleep. She felt depressed and upset. She hated hurting anyone and she knew that Chris had been hurt. She had been thoughtless tonight, though it was the only time she had offended. She felt she deserved a slap. The scent of the frangipani came to her and she opened the french windows and stepped out on to the veranda. The moon had gone in and the garden was a blackish-green jungle. Her gaze moved towards it and she walked along to the end of the veranda and down the side steps. The moon came out again then vanished behind the fretted silhouette that the treetops made against the midnight sky. The air was heavy with the musky sweet aroma of the blossoming trees and shrubs.

Something whirred by her ear with an indeterminate murmur. She was disturbed and aware and not surprised when she walked straight into Grant.

"My dear child, what are you doing out here?" He caught hold of her wrist.

"The same as you, I imagine."

He shook her slightly. "Don't speak like that, Adrienne, I don't like it." She stood quietly beneath his hands. "Are you upset about Chris?"

178

How could he have guessed? She decided to bluff her way out of it. "Of course not, why on earth should I be?"

Grant was annoyed with her. "Why should you not be, my girl? You know darn well you were flirting with him tonight and we both know why."

"Oh, be bothered!" She flung away from him, but his grip on her tightened painfully.

"Stand still, Adrienne. I know you're upset. It was foolish of you to be so provocative. But you're very inexperienced, after all."

Inexperienced, was she? And immature and foolish and a child! Why did he bother with her? "You don't know a thing, Grant. Let me go, you bully!"

Grant pulled her into his arms and began kissing her. She struggled momentarily and was done for. He tangled his hand in her long hair and held her fast. Where there had been no stars before, they came out and rocketed across the sky. Adrienne closed her eyes to shut them out.

There was nothing in the world for her but Grant, and his mouth and his arms and the scent of him. Where did ecstasy begin? Did it start at your toes and shiver up to your head, or was a hammering in the head all along? A golden bubble danced behind her eyes and burst into a thousand fiery fragments as she fell with a splash into an emerald pond.

Grant released her abruptly. There was perspiration on her forehead. "Go into the house, Adrienne. This is madness." He turned her forcibly away from him.

By the time she was in her room, her breathing had eased. She undressed slowly in the darkness and got into bed. Somewhere in the night a cat wailed. A spasm of hysteria welled up in her. "I'm suffering," she told the inky darkness, and straightaway fell asleep.

CHAPTER TEN

UNEXPECTEDLY Grant had to go to Melbourne. A new wool compressor from New Zealand was being demonstrated to the Board. It represented a considerable mechanical achievement, compressing the size of the bales by half, making for easier packaging and handling.

Although Grant did not anticipate being away for more than a few days Adrienne was assailed by three successive sensations. First it seemed as though her heart would break at his absence, then she felt a sense of respite from his agitating presence and on top of it all a strong curiosity as to his activities, business apart, in the city.

Adrienne flung open the windows of the office and welcomed the sunshine. She thrust her head out and breathed in frangipani. Their promise had barely begun to be fulfilled. The sun dazzled behind giant blue gums where it would sink in crimson splendour.

Adrienne turned back to her work, determined to keep her mind on it and nothing else. She was making a half-hearted attempt to do the filing when Grant came through to the office.

He gave her a keen glance. "Everything straightforward here, Adrienne?"

She hesitated, then shook her head. "I can't read your writing on that Ferguson letter." She said it without meeting his gaze, the colour coming to her cheeks. She could at a pinch make it out, but she felt the need to hang on to him.

Grant took it from her. "There's nothing out of the ordinary here. I think you just want to detain me."

Her voice was stilted. "Yes, I suppose it was a foolish thing to say."

He gave her a grin. "You'd lift a mood of blackest depression, little one." He took her slender-pointed fingers. The soft colour seemed to ebb and flow beneath her satiny skin. Nothing was said between them. The scent of summer breathed in through the window. A wasp alighted on the sill, crawled along an inch or two, then droned through the room. Adrienne ducked instinctively and Grant picked up a white square of paper, made a swipe with it and the black and gold comet dived out the door.

Adrienne stood very still. Gauzy trails of heat spiralled round her head and she heard Grant's voice from afar off. "There's something bothering you, I can see, but I haven't much time. I'm cutting it fine as it is." His gaze rested on the tender curve of her neck. "Look after yourself until I get back."

He walked to the door, then turned. Her delicate profile was silhouetted against the morning glow. He didn't think he was mistaken – there was the sparkle of tears on her lashes. He came back into the room. "I might as well make it my fourth major offence." Her breath came in a long gasp as Grant tipped back her head and found her mouth, closing on its softness with complete possession. She seemed to fold into him and he drew her hard up against him, encircling her throat with his hand. Her heart flew through her lips.

"Tomorrow I may be myself with yesterday's seven thousand years." The bellbird started to chime in her head.

Grant put her away from him. He was smiling. "Surely you understand what this means?"

Her eyes opened wide in instant comprehension. "You don't want me as your secretary."

Grant brushed back her hair. "Good God, Adrienne, I'll have to stop talking to you altogether!" He shot back his cuff. "I shouldn't be here." He looked at Adrienne. She was regarding him with an expression of drama. "Promise me something, Adrienne."

"What is it, Grant?" Her face clouded over.

"Leave all your feverish fancies alone until I get back, like a good girl. Promise me?"

181

"Feverish fancies—" So he knew about them! "Yes, Grant," she answered quietly.

He patted her cheek and went out. She didn't see his expression. It was one of extreme tenderness.

The big day dawned like any other with a curious lack of originality. Adrienne lay face down on the pillow. No wonder the kookaburra laughed; he was making mock of her. Grant had not returned. He had sent a brief telegram – "Unexpectedly delayed – will make it." One guess as to the cause of his delay. If he came with Prue Gowan she would faint on the lawn. No, she would laugh and talk and bet wildly on the horses and come back and pack her bags.

The first race was timed for eleven-thirty and there were to be seven races, the last scheduled to go off at four-ten p.m. The household was ready at ten-thirty a.m. Mrs. Manning had chosen a mint-cool coin-spotted dress and matching jacket with a wide-brimmed white sombrero. Lyla sported a stunning round-the-clock ensemble in pink satin linen, her hair completely covered by organdie cherry blossom. She carried a matching parasol. Adrienne didn't care how she looked, though her subconscious attention to detail turned her out very elegantly indeed in an avocado silk dress with a matching cut-away jacket and a burnt orange straw breton. Mrs. Manning gave her a swift glance of approval. She looked very chic and very lovely.

The racecourse was four miles out of the town and boasted the longest straight in the country. It was very pretty, set in the middle of pine-covered hills. Evidently children were not barred from the track, for they were everywhere – racing, jumping somersaulting on the lawn, thundering through the members' stand.

Already the boots of the cars were open and collapsible tables and chairs set up on the lawn. For once Adrienne wasn't hungry. She wended her way through tea in a thermos and cordial for the kids, past the beer and sandwiches, and on to the chicken and champagne. The bigger

182

the car the bigger the boot and the more lavish the picnic basket. For a wealthy woman Lyla was a cautious gambler. She had allowed herself ten dollars – the same amount in fact as Adrienne – and fully expected to treble it by the end of the afternoon. No doubt she would.

Desolately Adrienne picked at the breast of chicken, she disliked eating when she was dressed up anyway. Mrs. Manning was saying to Lyla, "If it's humanly possible he'll be here."

The horses paraded along the fence and Lyla became very knowledgeable. Adrienne's heart was in her avocado shoes. Nevertheless she placed her first bet, a dollar each way on the frisky one.

"You'll have to be more specific, little lady."

Adrienne consulted her book. "Number three, Midnight Kiss," then she gulped. That was an omen – Midnight Kiss flew in. Adrienne interrupted her soul-searching to collect. By the beginning of the fifth race she had a small following. Her bets were all in terms of "to win" or "on the nose". Mindless of the result she backed four straight winners. Midnight Kiss – My Surprise – Local Choice – and Times Up. They all had a bearing on the immediate situation. She wasn't interested in form, a hard track or the ground easy. Anything that seemed relevant she backed. She now had forty-five dollars crumpled up in her bag.

In a fit of hopeless dejection, she put them on Liberty Girl's nose. Lyla was still talking youngsters and fillies and bold stayers and impressive breeding. Adrienne was having a little trouble shutting her bag. Marion and Chris, accompanied by a soignée young woman – who turned out to be Tammy – were having a cold beer from the back of the car.

Adrienne assumed a bright smile. "How's it going?"

They all seemed pleased to see her. "We've been looking all over for you, girl," Chris said. "Where've you been?"

Adrienne waved vaguely. "Oh, I've been round the ring."

Lyla's sharp eyes noticed the bulging bag. "With some success, I'd say!"

Miss Flower Face was a dark horse. Adrienne accepted a beer although she didn't care for it. That and the strong sun made her feel lightheaded. Everyone seemed to be dressed in blue or white. She set down her empty glass and returned to the ring while they gazed after her wonderingly.

"I didn't know Adrienne was a racegoer." Chris seemed surprised. Marion guessed correctly that Adrienne didn't know where she was going without Grant.

It was a perfect racing day, fine and cloudless with a fast track. Everyone seemed to be enjoying themselves immensely, win or lose. Chris insisted on taking the two girls to afternoon tea in the pavilion. Adrienne ate gaily. God knows how I'm suffering, she thought. She gazed out of the plate glass window on to the moving heads of the crowd.

"It's a pity Grant's been delayed," Chris was saying. "Something important must have cropped up."

Adrienne smiled and nodded through the pleasant chit-chat. "Thank you for the afternoon tea, Chris, I've enjoyed it. I must fly, though, if I want to get on to the next race. Excuse me, you two." Tammy started to laugh. She would never have thought Adrienne such a gambler!

Merry Madam won the sixth and Quick Flight the last. Adrienne had picked the programme.

The races were over and all thoughts were on the ball, which was to begin a eight-thirty. The last winner and a telegram from her father advising her to enjoy herself decided Adrienne. She went to Mrs. Manning with a pale hand to her head. "Tonight of all nights and my stepmother has been taken ill! I'll have to go to her." Heaven forgive me for lying!

Mrs. Manning was all sympathy. "My dear, I'm so sorry. Is there anything I can do?"

Adrienne smiled mutely. It was the only time Linda had ever come in handy. "There's a bus through town at six-thirty, isn't there?"

Mrs. Manning was perturbed at the suddenness of the flight. She had wrongly concluded, it would seem, that Adrienne wasn't on good terms with her stepmother. "Oh, Adrienne, I do wish you didn't have to go, but that's just being selfish of me. If you must, you must."

In the middle of packing a small suitcase, Adrienne was overcome by laughter. She heard it from afar off. "I must be hysterical," she thought. "I would be if I saw Grant walk in with his party of friends." She had made a fool of herself long enough. Her behaviour had been shameless, and flight was the only solution. At least her pride or what remained of it would be salvaged. She would live from minute to minute, working on a plan as it occurred to her. "What about Marion's painting?" she asked herself aloud. "I can't think about it now. *Che sara, sara.*"

They all saw her off. It was an affectionate farewell, and even Lyla was seen to blink. Adrienne waved through the bus window in despair. Her face had a solemn, secret look touched with sadness. The dark eyes mirrored past rapture, present pain. The bus pulled out of the town and she stared unseeingly at the pale imperfect blue of the evening sky. The distant trees were a smoky lilac and the breeze through the open window blew in the elusive aromatic scent of the bush. The highway snaked on for ever, and after a while she slept.

Linda was unbecomingly pregnant and disgustingly healthy. She accepted Adrienne's story of having a few days off and on that account managed to be gracious, after her own fashion. Her father was surprised but delighted. He too accepted, "If you've been to one ball, you've been to them all." Approaching second fatherhood had dulled his perception.

Adrienne had changed for the better, Linda decided. She was quiet and introspective and seemed genuinely concerned regarding Linda's worn condition. In actual fact both women had mellowed. Adrienne was now wholly engrossed with her own personal problem and Linda had gained the confidence and equanimity of achieved, or soon to be, womanhood. A state of truce prevailed.

On the Wednesday evening Adrienne went into the Town Hall to hear the Symphony Orchestra give a Czech concert under a visiting Czech baton. She sank into an end seat; the situation was getting beyond her.

Twenty minutes before the interval as the audience applauded Smetana Adrienne felt her elbow firmly grasped. She turned and her lips moved soundlessly. "Come along, Adrienne, we can't wait for the interval." She was forced to follow him. An attendant sprang to the door solicitiously. The young lady must have come over faint. She had arrived alone – he had noticed her especially. One didn't see such a pretty girl without an escort. Well, she had one now, a handsome big bloke too. What would you expect? He shut the door after them. He had done his dash.

Grant compelled her down the front steps and out to the car park. He was just unlocking the car with one hand, the other still retaining a grip on her wrist, when Adrienne found her voice rather imperiously. "What's the meaning of this, Grant?"

He put her into the car, almost too exasperated to answer. "Once and for all, Adrienne, I'm doing the questioning." He switched on the ignition and the big car purred to life. Grant drove in silence out of the city and pulled into a sheltered promontory overlooking the harbour. Moonlight sheened across the water, trailing a glory and increasing Adrienne's feeling of heartbreak. Her face had a haunted longing look touched with flashes of excitement. Grant was Grant at any price. He flicked on the interior lights and turned towards her, his eyes intense to the point of anger.

"Perhaps you'll explain your crazy flight and the extraordinary nonsense you've been handing out to everyone." He held up an irritable hand. "Before you do I might

186

mention that I've seen your father and he told me where to find you."

Adrienne was aghast. "What on earth did you say to them?" Her voice trailed helplessly.

"I said I was hoping to find you at home – what else could I say? I think your daughter is a harmless lunatic. Helen told me about Linda's attack. She was blooming on Friday night when I saw her, so I rather doubted that. Really, Adrienne, just how much do you think I can take?"

Adrienne was distressed. "Why don't you say it? Go on, say it, you're a fool!" She looked and sounded so agitated that Grant smiled a little despite himself.

"Well, you are a little foolish, Adrienne, but I'm dedicated to saving your flower face. Just tell me what it's all about."

Adrienne drew a deep breath and looked out the window. The moon was white tonight, haloed by a silver beauty. Soon it would be Christmas. Why was the moonlight different at Christmas, more white, more mysterious, more romantic? She cleared her throat.

Grant reached out to her fiercely and pulled her into his arms. "Would it make it any easier, silly, sweet Adrienne, if I told you I loved you and wanted you and feared to leave you out of my sight?"

Her eyes filled with tears. "Oh, Grant, how extraordinary! I feel exactly the same way. But why did you stay away?"

"Oh, stay away be damned!" Grant was tired and exasperated. He had driven goodness knows how many miles and was unwilling to go into the whys and the wherefores so dear to the hearts of the best of women.

"Say what you want to say," she murmured, anxious to meet him half-way.

"Good lord, child, I've just said it. I'm not in a talking mood anyway." He bent his head and found her mouth, silencing her completely.

Adrienne uttered a soft cry, and the quality of his lovemaking changed. Fire crackled along her nerve centres. She felt soft and weak and overcome by a spasm of surging emotion – "Help me, I'm drowning!"

Grant lifted his head, maintaining a dangerous control. There were tears on her cheeks and he brushed them away gently. "I didn't mean to hurt you, my love, but you make it very hard for me." He drew her head on to his shoulder.

"I think I've been too impulsive," she said. "I thought you were in love with Prue Gowan."

Grant felt incredulous. He was dead tired, definitely frustrated, and here she was, the love of his life, indulging in far-fetched nonsense! He shook his head slightly.

Adrienne watched him keenly. "You needn't be afraid to tell me. I like the truth."

He rubbed his eyes with the back of his hand. "My darling girl, I'm touched by your understanding heart, but I've nothing to tell you. I've never met the lady, heaven help me."

"I hope so," she smiled, an enormous crushing burden lifted from her spirit. She touched a finger to the cleft in his chin. Grant moved and the night folded over them. There was silence for a long time.

"You're trembling, my darling." Dark eyes could be the brightest of mirrors. Grant looked down at her. This has been inevitable from the first moment he saw her. Sensations moved through him in sweet lazy waves. Together there would be days like honey, all golden and tangible and nights when the world would explode with fire and the times in between he could handle. He breathed in the air laden with scent of her.

Elation rose swiftly in him. Adrienne stirred in his arms, unwilling to move from their strength and safety. "Oh, Grant, you will take me back to Saranga?"

He put her from him filled with decision. "Where else would I take you, my love? If we hurry we'll catch the last of the jacaranda."

Mills & Boon Classics

The very best of Mills and Boon
romances, brought back for those of you
who missed reading them when they
were first published.

There are three other Classics for you to collect this
December

THE SILVER SLAVE
by Violet Winspear

The imposing Dom Duarte de Montqueiro Ardo thought
that Rosary was too young and inexperienced to tutor his
daughter. And that wasn't the only problem.

TANGLE IN SUNSHINE
by Rosalind Brett

Tessa instantly resented David Clavering, but as she grew to
know him better, she found herself hoping that he might
not be too deeply attracted to her cousin Raine.

LEGACY OF THE PAST
by Anne Mather

The two men in Madeline's life so far had been gentle and
kind. Nicholas Vitale was anything but gentle — but
Madeline couldn't resist him . . .

If you have difficulty in obtaining any of these books from
your local paperback retailer, write to:

Mills & Boon Reader Service
P.O. Box 236, Thornton Road, Croydon, Surrey, CR9 3RU

The Mills & Boon Rose is the Rose of Romance

Every month there are ten new titles to choose from — ten new stories about people falling in love, people you want to read about, people in exciting, far away places. Choose Mills & Boon. It's your way of relaxing.

December's titles are:

TEMPLE OF THE DAWN by *Anne Hampson*
Lexa lost her heart to Paul Mansell — but his heart belonged, as it always would, to his beautiful dead wife Sally . . .

MY DARLING SPITFIRE by *Rosemary Carter*
The only way Siane could join her fiancé on a remote game reserve was to go in the company of the *maddening* André Connors!

KONA WINDS by *Janet Dailey*
Happy in her teaching job in Hawaii, Julie then met her pupil's grim half-brother . . .

BOOMERANG BRIDE by *Margaret Pargeter*
Four years ago, when Vicki was expecting her husband Wade's child, he had thrown her out. So why was he now forcing her to return?

SAVAGE INTERLUDE by *Carole Mortimer*
James St Just was Kate's half-brother, but Damien Savage didn't know that, and he had jumped to all the wrong conclusions . . .

THE JASMINE BRIDE by *Daphne Clair*
Rachel didn't think it mattered that she was so much younger than Damon Curtis — but she was also very much more inexperienced . . .

CHAMPAGNE SPRING by *Margaret Rome*
The arrogant Marquis de la Roque thought the worst of Chantal and her brother — but she was determined to prove him wrong!

DEVIL ON HORSEBACK by *Elizabeth Graham*
Joanne went as housekeeper to Alex Harper — but he was convinced that she was only yet another candidate for the position of his wife . . .

PRINCE OF DARKNESS by *Susanna Firth*
After five years' separation from her husband Elliott, Cassie was just about getting over it when Elliott turned up again — as her boss.

COUNTRY COUSIN by *Jacqueline Gilbert*
Eleanor liked most of the Mansel family. What a pity she couldn't feel the same way about one of them, the uncompromising Edward . . .

If you have difficulty in obtaining any of these books from your local paperback retailer, write to:

Mills and Boon Reader Service
P.O. Box No 236, Thornton Road, Croydon, Surrey CR9 3RU.

Mills & Boon Classics

The very best of Mills and Boon
romances, brought back for those of you who
missed reading them when they
were first published

and in
January
we bring back the following four
great romantic titles.

THE SPELL OF THE ENCHANTER *by Margery Hilton*
Jo needed to enlist the help of Sir Sheridan Leroy, but
little did she expect that Sir Sheridan in his turn would
demand *her* help to further his own personal intrigue . . .

THE LITTLE NOBODY *by Violet Winspear*
Ynis had lost her memory in an accident, so she had to
believe the dark and mysterious Gard St. Clair when he
said that she was going to marry him . . .

MAN OUT OF REACH *by Lilian Peake*
When Rosalie asked the new deputy head, Dr. Adrian
Crayford, why he couldn't tolerate women, he replied that
they were an irritating distraction, and the more attractive
they were, the greater distraction they became. And Rosalie
was attractive — and attracted to him!

WHITE ROSE OF WINTER *by Anne Mather*
It was six years since Julie had married Michael Pemberton
and left England — and Robert. Now Michael was dead, and
Julie and her small daughter were home again — only to
learn that Robert was now the child's guardian . . .

If you have difficulty in obtaining any of these books from
your local paperback retailer, write to:

Mills and Boon Reader Service
P.O. Box No 236, Thornton Road, Croydon, Surrey CR9 3RU

192